CATHERINE GILLING

Nothing is Simple

SOME STORIES ARE CLOSER TO HOME

Mereo Books

2nd Floor, 6-8 Dyer Street, Cirencester, Gloucestershire, GL7 2PF
An imprint of Memoirs Books. www.mereobooks.com
and www.memoirsbooks.co.uk

Nothing is Simple

ISBN: 978-1-86151-880-4

First published in Great Britain in 2022
by Mereo Books, an imprint of Memoirs Books.

A CIP catalogue record for this book is available from the British Library.

The address for Memoirs Books can be
found at www.mereobooks.com

Mereo Books Ltd. Reg. No. 12157152

Typeset in 11/16pt Plantin
by Wiltshire Associates.
Printed and bound in Great Britain

CHAPTER 1

Chris Page sighed deeply as he ran his fingers through his thick hair, flexed his tired shoulder muscles and settled into his aircraft seat. At last! The prospect of a peaceful escape from everything connected to his manic reporting job on a newspaper brought a smile to his face. The welcome boost of the early summer sun and blue skies had been long overdue. He did not give any thought to his colleagues in the office, Cherry and Alan, nor to the files which he knew would grow relentlessly on his desk during his absence. This well-deserved holiday would allow him to switch off completely from the chatter, noise and mayhem of work and London.

On the flight to Sardinia he listened to other passengers murmuring to themselves as they planned later trips out and about the island, while he made no plans at all. He was here to simply relax and enjoy each day as it came, to roam the quiet countryside, to swim and to lie on the beautiful, soft beaches of the southern shores. The wonderfully warm climate of the Cagliari coast, with its unspoilt natural surroundings, slower pace of life and magnificent scenery, promised to be exactly what he needed. He loved these lesser known places where he could observe people from a distance without having to talk to them. He had long developed the knack of recognising and avoiding those likely to have an unwelcome impact on his stay, the brash, the boastful and those full of bonhomie who wanted to make friends were kept at a safe distance. He did not mind appearing unsociable and melting into the background. Here, he preferred his own company, to please himself and to explore his surroundings on his own.

He spent the first few days mooching around the hotel and grounds unwinding before being drawn into taking one of the boat trips on offer. Like many of the other visitors he could not resist seeing the coast from a different perspective. He spent an idyllic afternoon on board, finding himself in tune with the other lazy holidaymakers who were stretched out or lulled to sleep by the soft chugging and gentle throb of the engine.

What he had not expected was for his gentle repose on the deck to be painfully and suddenly shattered when his shins received a severe blow. His initial yelp was accompanied by an audible gasp from those around him as the person who had tripped over his legs ended up sprawled at his feet.

Quickly with-drawing his bruised limbs and rubbing his shins, he discovered himself facing a female who was down on her hands and knees. With her long hair now hanging forward over her face, she looked like a shaggy dog. He had trouble hiding a smirk as the woman flung back a mass of dark hair to glare at him before turning herself into a sitting position to gingerly examine her own injuries.

"Are you all right? Let me help you up," he said, feeling genuine concern.

"Idiot!" she snapped angrily. She tossed back her head and her dark eyes flashed with condemnation.

"I'm sorry. Are you hurt?" He was still trying to dismiss that earlier image of a shaggy dog which had been so amusing. Luckily, she could not have realised the picture she had presented.

The girl struggled to her feet and brushed herself down, still ignoring his offered hand. "You don't own the deck! Sticking your legs out like that is a hazard," she told him, with another thunderous glare. His own blue eyes flared back at her unreasonable attitude. For goodness sake! It was simply a silly accident, these things happen. Half of it was her own fault anyway, wasn't she looking where she was going. He resented her determination to place the blame totally on himself, but he was not going to get into an argument or cause an unpleasant scene. It wasn't worth it.

"OK, OK, it was my fault. What do you want? Damages?" he replied sarcastically, giving the merest flick of his raised eyebrows.

She did not retaliate, but merely stared at him. After a few minutes of petulant sulking she plodded cautiously along the deck in her canvas shoes towards the rear stairway. Chris shrugged dismissively and gave a little shake of the head before turning back to concentrate on the view once more. He was old and experienced enough not to let anything so trivial spoil his holiday mood.

Despite Chris's intention to take it easy on this holiday, laziness was not one of his traits. Having experienced the best of the hotel, he set out from the elegant lobby to enjoy a leisurely stroll down to the sea front. There he took an exhilarating swim, the sensation of the waves revitalizing his tired muscles and leading him to swim a little further than he had intended. He would be a little stiff tomorrow, but he could put up with that. He couldn't resist wiggling his toes in the sand and listening to the sound of the water splashing gently on the quiet beach. How was it that something so simple made him smile?

Today he felt utterly content. He stretched out his towel and sat in the warm sun to restore his faded tan, idly people-watching for a while. Then he picked up his battered paperback and turned over onto his front to let his back feel the sun. He managed one more chapter before turning over again. He had no intention of getting burnt in the direct midday sun, however inviting it seemed. He had made that mistake when he was younger and had never forgotten the soreness or the pain. Having dried off, he headed back into the village for a drink, where he settled at one of the outside tables in the shade. The ambience of the surroundings seemed like another world and filled him with mellow satisfaction.

As he savoured the moment, a figure across the square caught his attention. Surely not? He must be mistaken. In fact it took him several glances before he accepted it had to be her again – the woman from the boat. He sipped his beer, hoping she would soon wander off out of sight. He did not expect her to recognise him, but he would prefer it if she didn't. While he had almost forgotten about yesterday and put it out of his mind, there was no guarantee that she would be so obliging. Past experience naturally made him cautious of assuming anything where women were concerned. With other female acquaintances and two sisters as prime examples, he never took anything for granted.

Yet it was hardly inconvenient to have her invade his view for a moment. He did not own the place. No doubt she was simply another tourist on one of the organised day trips. She and the rest of them would soon head back to the little tour buses parked at the harbour and be gone.

He finished his drink and began the long, slow walk up the hill back to the hotel. There were stunning views on every side, and he stopped several times to take it all in. It was truly beautiful; no wonder Cherry had recommended it.

He arrived back at the hotel entrance at the same time as the local shuttle bus that had come up from the village. The bus was not that full, with only a few people disembarking.

The last person leapt off the bus to skip across the forecourt and into the hotel with an air of carefree enjoyment. It was the woman with the dark hair again. What was she doing here? But then logic kicked in; she was only here to dine, as an extra option on her package day out. With the mouth-watering choices on the menu, he could not blame her. She would not be disappointed.

His curiosity satisfied, he discreetly made his way past the front desk and went to shower and change. Refreshed, he sauntered through the lounge and out into the rear garden to indulge in coffee and cake while he considered his choices for the evening.

He was still deliberating when the girl passed right by him and walked out of the private back gate. He watched her walk away along the cliff path nearby, heading purposefully off into the distance. He was thankful that she was not one of his fellow guests. He did not really want to keep on bumping into her on a regular basis.

That evening found Chris at the information desk in the hotel lobby, studying the postcards – he would have to send some at some point during his stay – and browsing through the tours on offer. He considered the mountainous interior and ancient ruins, but could not be bothered in the end. Nothing had instantly appealed. He would probably mooch about again locally, as he had done today. Unless something completely different sprang to mind.

The next day, in a completely mad moment, it did. He

suddenly decided to stop being so lazy and to try to make better use of his free time. He would hire one of those unfamiliar mountain bikes. He was going to make a fool of himself, no doubt, but who would notice his inexperience? He would begin on the deserted roads outside the village, where he could not come to much harm. What were a few bruises anyway?

With no one around to notice him, he cautiously and apprehensively set off. Spurred on by a ridiculous sense of adventure, he carefully pedalled along the very quiet lanes, gently weaving from side to side to keep his balance. It was not that easy. Why was he doing this? He was no sportsman. But he was not going to give up. If he pedalled faster, would the speed keep him in a straight line?

So, risking life and limb on the bumpy, uneven surface, he gave it a go. It seemed to work, but then, as he was approaching the first sharp bend, disaster struck. He panicked and braked too hard, to find himself swerving, churning up the gravel and skidding to a sudden stop. He almost fell off the bike as it went sideways from under him, but somehow he managed to finish standing on his feet, still holding the handlebars of the tilted frame between his legs. He felt quite shaky and his legs were trembling.

Then he looked up to find himself only inches from a woman, some poor pedestrian he had not even noticed before, who had been forced to jump out of the way. She was sitting in a hedge. Heavens, what had he done?

Throwing the bike to the ground, he rushed over to

make sure she was all right, gushing sincere words of regret and hoping she understood English. Half-expecting a tirade of Italian in return, which he would not understand, he was not prepared for his victim to be the person she was, out of all the people on the island. That woman again. His apologies were met with a brief, horrified silence before the young woman gave full vent to her feelings.

"You again! You are not safe to be let out on your own!" she yelled at him.

She pushed herself out of the hedge and began picking the leaves and twigs off of her clothing, grunting and throwing them to the ground in fury. Finally she brushed herself down.

"I'm sorry, I couldn't help it," he muttered weakly. "I'm a little rusty. I haven't been on a bike for years."

"Rusty! I should think you are!"

He was unwilling to risk a confrontation with her. Although he deserved the criticism, he wanted to divert her annoyance. He accepted that this fresh encounter called for a touch of diplomacy. He was usually quite good at that.

"My name is Chris Page. I'm staying at the hotel at the top of the hill," he told her.

"Really? I must remember to avoid it"

Avoid it? Fat chance! He had seen her on several occasions. She seemed to be roaming in and out of the hotel whenever it suited her, with no apparent purpose.

"I think we have already met," he sighed, despite knowing it was a mistake.

"As if I could forget," she murmured under her breath.

He was stumped for a response, not that it mattered.

She turned away from him with-out any further acknowledgement, which probably, on reflection, was just as well, he thought. Her departure saved him the embarrassment of having to ride off in front of her and prove his utter incompetence again. Not that he had the energy to do that either.

In fact, he needed to gather himself together. There were moments when he should accept that he wasn't a fit young lad any more. Let's face it, the only exercise, if you could call it that, he took these days was the occasional swimming, game of tennis or pitch and putt with two friends. He was in his mid-thirties and had not participated in any sort of strenuous activity for a long time before today. He really did need someone to curb these odd bursts of rashness. Ellen had been his mentor as well as the woman in his life, but she was away on a research expedition and had been for a long, long time, and he had no way of knowing when she would return. He missed her desperately, but he had had to get used to that.

He took a deep breath and got up. He would have to walk back pushing the bike, because his limbs were still trembling as a result of the fall. He dragged himself along, definitely feeling demoralised, but thankful that the altercation had not been worse. They were both in one piece.

By the time he had had lunch and a much-needed rest

to recuperate, his mood had improved and he was feeling much better. He refused to be deterred by the incident; it had not been that bad, he convinced himself. In fact, having regained some of his confidence, he felt determined not to give up so easily. He would give it another try.

Over the next few days, Chris persisted with his challenge to master the mountain bike and was beginning to enjoy this new experience. As he criss-crossed the narrow, meandering lanes and explored the empty cliff top, he discovered a host of hidden gems in the area. There were some truly charming homes peacefully tucked away amongst the coastal scenery, family homes preserved by generations of care and devotion, that were so attractive that he could not resist peering curiously over the fences and hedges on route.

There was one in particular he found quite stunning. It was a beautiful white secluded villa, set in a brilliant garden bursting with colourful plants. He stared at it for ages, soaking up the detail and not wanting to leave. He sighed appreciatively. It was captivating. A picture of it deserved to be in every glossy magazine, although he doubted the owner would appreciate the publicity. To think this was some one's private home. How lucky they were!

Nevertheless he fumbled in his pockets for his digital camera, hoping to take a photo for Paula, his older sister. As a garden fanatic, she would adore this. But he could not find the camera. He patted his other pockets; still no joy. Wondering where else he might have put it, he ended up emptying everything from the small backpack he carried onto the ground and rummaging through the contents. It was not there. He must have left the camera in his room. A damn nuisance.

Still, it was not going to stop him coming back to capture this piece of perfection. He just hoped the owner would not be around to object when he did. So, throwing everything back into the bag, he dragged himself away to set off back on the bike towards the hotel.

He had not been riding for more than a few minutes when his nemesis appeared, approaching on foot from the opposite direction.

"What the devil are you doing here?" she snapped, her eyes narrowed suspiciously at him.

Chris frowned. What was it with this woman? What a cheek! What did it have to do with her, what he did or where he went? He felt like telling her what he thought of her, but resisted.

"I thought it would be safer for the general public," came his flippant reply.

But his little joke failed to impress her. She still seemed cross with him.

"This stretch of road is intended for the use of residents only," she informed him indignantly.

Chris refused to be made to feel in the wrong again for no good reason. No, he would not have it.

"Not actually private then?" he said tersely.

He could see she was not about to admit that, or say

anything else. She just stood there glaring. He took a slow breath. There was no point in letting this get out of hand.

"This is a delightful spot. Do you live around here?" he asked impulsively.

She looked him up and down, obviously niggled at this sudden unexpected personal question, then walked off down the lane without bothering to answer.

"Wait. Could I at least know your name?" he attempted, trying to be sociable.

"Good day, Mr Page," she said calmly, without turning round.

This time he was the one to shake his head, yet he had a sudden urge to get back at her. She was not going to have everything her own way. Damn her attitude! She had set him the challenge and he was determined to find out her name, simply because she had refused to give it. It would amuse him; besides, he was a reporter. It should not take him long. He would be satisfied to have one up on her.

He found her name easily; it was Francesca. He had not needed to ask anyone; he overheard it when she was talking at the front desk. She often lingered there, chatting animatedly with the staff as she passed through. He had not wanted to know more. He was content to let his interest drop, although her effortlessly switching from Italian back to English as required, depending upon whom she was talking to, had impressed him. Her accent was so perfect in both languages that it was difficult to tell her actual nationality. She must have been a tourist rep to be that good, he surmised. Not that it mattered precisely what or who she was.

Chris was quite happy to make the most of the sun and resume his lazy routine of lying on the beach, swimming and trying to finish his battered book in between his regular exercise on the bike. In fact he was determined to master this new ability so he could boast about it to his sisters and colleagues. He would never be another Chris Froome, but his sense of achievement, little as it was, made him proud of what he had done.

The next time he went out on the bike he knew he had pushed himself too hard, because when he stopped, all the muscles in his legs were shaking. Even his hands tingled because he had gripped the handlebars too tightly for too long. He propped the bike against the hedge and flopped down on the bank to recover his energy. Then with his stomach rumbling, obviously another cause for his flagging energy, he dived into his backpack for some food. He soon devoured his packed lunch and leaned back to let his body recover.

As he slowly sipped the remains of his bottled juice, he remembered he would soon have to think about finding an unusual and entertaining gift for his younger sister, Bridget. If he failed, his life would not be worth living; he always brought her something. He just was not sure what would match up to his previous presents. The hotel had suggested several places he should try for independent craft shops, but it could wait a few days longer. He was making the most of his last few precious days here, and he did not want to think of the holiday ending so soon.

From this inconspicuous and very quiet spot there was not much local activity to observe. A cart and then a truck passed, carrying rural workers on their way to the fields. Then nothing, until he witnessed a girl down the lane waving to someone else in the distance. Yes, it was the girl with the long dark hair again. Soon after he saw her throw herself into the arms of a man, and there followed an exuberant and long embrace. Chris smiled; a perfect example of the uninhibited nature of these Mediterranean types. They were oblivious to anything else. They walked on towards a car, the pair of them arm in arm, holding tightly to each other, with no attempt to hide their fondness for each other. How refreshing, he thought as he continued to watch them. How it reminded him of – well – moments in his earlier days. Those fond youthful memories he would never forget.

Naturally, he had not meant to take a good look at them as they drove past him minutes later; it had been merely curiosity, nothing more, he told himself. He did not even blink at the sight of her head leaning on his shoulder, but what did surprise him was her choice of companion. He was not some fine-featured Adonis, the sort of young, handsome red-blooded Italian male who would have been the perfect match for her. No, it was an older man with slightly greying temples who was behaving like some enduring Casanova, a Latin playboy, or worse. He smirked wickedly, delighted to imagine this spirited woman was involved with some dubious older man. Who would have thought it? But that was Italians for you. And today Francesca had proved herself to be typically Italian.

Chris headed back to the hotel, the earlier distraction forgotten. He really had to concentrate on finding Bridget her present. He wondered how she was getting on. No one had met her latest boyfriend yet, and she was a little reticent about admitting that the guy was on crutches. It all sounded very complicated. Chris only hoped it would work out for her.

He searched all the local craft and gift shops without success; nothing was good enough or different enough. With Bridget's interest in design, it had to be special and out of the ordinary, which meant it would be expensive as well.

As he continued his quest to please his sister, he occasionally caught sight of Francesca and her friend. Far from keeping a low profile, they were openly flaunting their passion. Indeed, their easy, lilting laughter hinted at a long-established relationship. He briefly wondered what her family thought about their liaison. He would not have liked it if his sister had been behaving in that manner, puritan that he was.

On the hotel's recommendation, he decided to visit the town of Pula, with its traditional narrow winding streets, shops and restaurants, having been assured that he would find a wider choice of gift shops there. He spent an interesting morning exploring the town, and it took him a while to decide on what to buy. Then, with the precious glass gift beautifully wrapped, he carried it carefully in its designer bag back to the hotel and had a coffee while he waited in the foyer for the shuttle bus to take him back to his own hotel.

He had only sat down for a moment when the man he had seen canoodling with Francesca walked past. Chris glanced quickly about to see if she was also around, but then the conversation at the front desk took his full attention.

"Your wife and children are in the lounge, sir. Are you all dining here tonight?" the clerk asked in perfect English.

The man nodded and disappeared briefly, to re-appear with an elegant dark-haired woman and two teenage children, all of them merrily chattering together. They presented the picture of a typical Italian happy family, as he proudly escorted them to the chauffeur-driven car drawing up outside.

Chris stood up as they drove off. So, Francesca's paramour was a married man! No wonder she was so feisty; she clearly had no qualms about what she was doing. This independent woman was obviously no saint and was thoroughly enjoying the romantic attention of this older man. Well, well, she was a dark horse.

He finished his coffee, then, unable to contain his curiosity any longer, he went over to the hotel receptionist. He could not help the investigative journalist in him. He enquired casually about the distinctive-looking guest who had just left. The woman instantly beamed back; she was obviously proud that this man spent every summer here together with his wife and children. His name was Oliviero Savante. Apparently the arrangement had been ongoing for decades. The family were valued clients and this part of Sardinia was almost their second home.

On his journey back to the host resort, Chris could not help being fascinated by what he had discovered. He chuckled. Francesca and this married man! Although he did not know her, he had somehow expected better of her. But maybe this free-spirited female and her mature seducer deserved each other.

But this was nothing to do with him. He was not at work now.

The last couple of days of his holiday were wonderful. Totally relaxed, he lay in the sun and listened to the sound of the waves. He picnicked on the cliff tops and swam in the crystal clear turquoise waters. There was nothing to intrude into his comfortable blissful indulgence.

All too soon it was his next to last day, and he had one task to do before he left tomorrow. He had to get back to that white villa to take some photos for Paula. He checked the camera was safely in his pocket this time and set off. He had returned the bike to the hire place and it was a pleasant walk along the back of the hotel. It had not taken long. There it was exactly as he remembered, if not even more glorious.

He leant over the wooden garden gate. The garden seemed very English, he thought, now he had time to study it properly. A lawn flowed between the shrubs and trees of its boundary. He gazed around, checking if he could see anyone about the place. All was quiet and deserted, so he took his chance before anyone suddenly turned up. He quickly snapped away, taking as many pictures as he could of the villa and the abundant rich colours of the garden. Then he stuffed the camera back in his pocket like a guilty schoolboy. None of the neighbours had shouted out, so he felt safe to linger for one last gaze. Then he walked back to the hotel to settle in the garden with a cold beer to enjoy what was left of his last few hours here.

He had hardly sat down with his drink in the shade when from nowhere Francesca strode into sight, heading straight for him. She stopped and unexpectedly plonked herself down in a chair to sit opposite him. She leaned forward, glaring grimly at him.

Chris was beginning to sense more trouble. Why had she sought him out?

"I thought you were simply on holiday like everyone else," she said.

"I am. For goodness sake, what on earth have I done wrong this time?"

"You pretend to act innocent, but you are not. You can't be trusted."

"Sorry? Exactly what are you accusing me of?" he asked quietly.

"You were in Pula asking questions about one of the people staying there. The hotel community does not like our clients being pestered by unnecessary attention."

Pestered! How had he pestered anyone? He put his tongue in his cheek, a habit he had when trying to decide whether to speak or not, and scrutinized her. Was she worth the effort? He continued to eye her, eye to eye. How dare she criticize him when he had not done anything wrong.

"Excuse me, but you should get your facts straight before you start getting on your high horse," he said. "If you care to check. I was merely passing the time of day in reception, in normal conversation while I waited for the shuttle bus. There was no hidden agenda. No inquisition."

"You're a reporter!" she condemned him, through gritted teeth.

"Is that a crime?" Chris was not about to make excuses for his profession. He certainly did not have to justify himself to this person.

"No one deserves to be targeted by the press. We value our clients. They come here to relax and enjoy our hospitality."

"Which was exactly why I had come here! I hadn't expected to be pestered either, by you. I am also a guest here as well, you know. I think I deserve the same consideration, as everyone else? Don't you?" She ignored his curt retort. "As for being targeted by the press, what rubbish. Don't you think you are being a little too over protective? Anyone would think he is something special. Or does he have something to hide?" he added a little sarcastically.

"There is nothing here to interest you," she declared.

Chris did not stand any nonsense at work, and he was not

inclined to let her have the last word now. He didn't intend to cause a commotion, but he had had enough of staying polite. It was time to retaliate, time to rattle her composure.

"How can you be so sure? You're making me think there's something about him that's worth investigating."

He had been sorely tempted to say something he would regret. But why bother? He was getting fed up. It was obvious this conversation had run its course; it had nowhere left to go.

"As it is, all I want to do is finish this drink in peace and enjoy what is left of my last few hours in Sardinia. If you wouldn't mind," he snapped.

Francesca jumped to her feet and marched away without a further word. Not even a 'sorry' for that hostile attitude of hers. Women! He pulled a rueful face, glad she had gone. Glad that this would be the last he would see of her.

The next morning, he handed in his key and settled his bill. The staff member serving him leaned over, confidentially lowering her voice.

"Did Miss Lawson find you yesterday?"

"Who is Miss Lawson?" Chris asked, thinking it might be some other guest.

"Francesca. The hotel owner's relation."

So that explained her connection to the hotel. Well, well. He had not worked that one out.

"Oh yes she did. Thank you," he replied without going into detail.

"She did not seem very pleased with you," came the whisper.

"No. It's unfortunate. We got off to a bad start almost as soon as I arrived."

"I hope she didn't spoil your stay?"

She sounded quite concerned. Did they think he would print something detrimental on his return to London? No doubt they would not like any bad publicity reflected on their hotel. Should he put their minds at rest? He was not a travel critic. Although it suddenly seemed a good idea; maybe he could diversify into writing a personal travel journal column, if the paper would let him. No, realistically that was doubtful. Here he was getting side-tracked by that grasshopper mind of his. Back to the present. Chris smiled a cheerful convincing smile.

"No, she did not. On reflection, it was entertaining. I'll certainly have plenty of amusing tales to tell my friends when I get home. Miss Lawson will be a talking point for several days."

The girl looked quite shocked. Or was that real worry on her face? It was time to throw in one final remark, for prosperity. It had to be said; Francesca needed to be put in her place.

"In my opinion Miss Lawson – Francesca – has an unpredictable personality and is too free with her opinions. I did not appreciate her unfounded accusations. Her assumptions were utterly wrong. Not that I received any apology from her. That would be too much to expect, although I would have thought she owed me that much. You can tell her that if you like."

Diplomatically the girl at the desk refrained from any comment.

He picked up his case and joined the others on the coach for the journey to the airport. That was another holiday experience over. He sighed. Too soon he would be back in London and putting his mind back into work mode. Where had the time gone?

CHAPTER 2

As the plane began to circle over London to land, Chris was wondering what had occurred in his absence. The pulsating newsrooms of Fleet Street would never be short of material in this manic, noisy and overcrowded city. And he was part of that curious breed of journalists who spent their time interviewing and researching items for public consumption.

He arrived home from the airport and dumped his suitcase in the hall to be met by the sight of the same clutter in front of him which had been stacked on the floor for months. He pulled a face at the pile of decorating items in front of him. The tins of paint and undercoat remained untouched in the corner with the neatly folded dust sheet, sandpaper, brushes and cleaning stuff. The idea had been that if he left them there, it would force him to actually start painting the tatty looking bathroom, but so far it hadn't worked. The messy prospect of sanding down the woodwork had always been the perfect deterrent, to put him off even beginning. It was a standing joke at work. His colleagues had even taken bets on when he would get around to it.

Well, it would not be this week either, he acknowledged. He swiftly emptied the suitcase, throwing everything onto the bed or in the wash. Then he gave the case a good wipe over ready to take it back to his sister Bridget, from whom he had borrowed it, together with her present.

The precious gift was beautifully wrapped in its designer bag and he could not wait to see how much she liked it. He had taken such care over its choice, exploring the town, searching all the local craft and gift shops for something special and out of the ordinary, before deciding.

Once showered and changed, he set off across town, arriving at her place south of the river a few hours later. But for once, her welcoming smile did not have the brightness he was used to.

He made no comment as he followed her into the kitchen for their routine catch-up chat and carefully placed the present on the table. And there it sat untouched for a while. He was disappointed and puzzled by his sister's lack of enthusiasm. Normally she could not wait to tear the paper apart to see the contents with the childish excitement he always loved to see. Her eyes would widen with pleasure and she would beam at him as she examined each new gift he gave her.

She lifted it cautiously out of the smart designer bag before pulling the paper slowly off to reveal the dazzling coloured glass dish. She held it up to examine it against the light and smiled weakly before expressing her rather lame thanks and giving him the obligatory kiss on the cheek.

Chris frowned. This was not like her at all. He let her potter about the kitchen for a few minutes, before coming up to her and gently nudging her.

"Come on, tell me what's wrong. I'm a good listener."

She leaned into his warm, comforting hold, but said nothing. He was puzzled. Surely it was nothing to do with the new design venture she had set up with her friend. He knew Bridget was enjoying the variety of their assignments and the business was financially sound and attracting many clients. Her reluctance to discuss whatever was bothering her was clear, but as a caring brother he did not give up easily. Softly, softly was his approach. If he could start her talking about her creative passion, which had always been her favourite topic anyway, he might get somewhere.

"You're not having second thoughts about your business, are you?" he said, although he knew the answer before he asked.

She shook her head. "Of course not!" she said. At which, her mind now diverted, she began to enthuse about the recent exhibition publicity, to prove their success. He listened to her without interrupting until she had finished. She was almost back to normal, but not quite.

"You're not your usual perky self. Come on, tell me what's upset you."

Bridget screwed up her nose and pouted. "There's nothing to tell. I'm just feeling sorry for myself. I'm just being silly. It's nothing."

"You are never silly," he told her.

The probable cause suddenly clicked – the boyfriend. Heck! Chris didn't know much about the latest boyfriend, except from the odd comment she had mentioned. She did not share such personal details with a brother. Why would she? His tactful policy was not to get involved or ever offer advice. He would be no help in such matters. He did not have the feminine instinct to say the right things, he left that to Paula, their older married sister. All he could do was give her a comforting shoulder and a cuddle when she needed it. And today it seemed, she clearly needed both.

Later, as they laid the table ready to eat, he began to tell her about his holiday, in an attempt to lighten her mood. What else could he do? He had no choice. He started by proudly announcing his new skills with a mountain bike, at which she was highly doubtful. She could not imagine him on a bike, or keeping up such a hobby, and thought it would be no use in the dangerous London traffic. He pretended to be hurt by her comments, but she could see he was faking the response.

And then, even though he had not meant to, he related

the encounter where the woman had ended up in the hedge. Naturally he embellished it to make it as funny as he could. It worked perfectly and she was soon laughing and teasing him about the silly incident. This was the old Bridget, the one he knew and loved.

"I can't believe you. You're not safe to go on holiday on your own," she teased.

Chris smirked at her. He preferred to go on holidays on his own these days. It was habit, he could please himself, he could be utterly selfish. That was not about to change. Once away he could allow himself to wallow in fond memories of previous long summer holidays, wondering if the woman who had shared his life was still wandering the globe.

The conversation lulled while they ate their meal.

"Are you still seeing Matt?" Chris queried innocently, while she washed and he dried the dishes.

"For some reason he has been a little distant these past few weeks," Bridget responded, without offering any more information.

Chris knew when to drop the subject.

Later that evening, he finally got round to phoning Paula.

"You're back. How was the holiday?" she began cheerfully.

"Fine. I have some great photos of gardens for you. I'll put them in the post."

"Brilliant."

He went on to explain that he was really phoning her

because of Bridget. She had seemed so down when he had seen her earlier.

Paula laughed softly, one of those gentle familiar laughs, betraying her inside knowledge of the situation. These siblings rarely kept secrets from each other.

"If it's something delicate…" he began.

"No, no. To be honest, it's nothing to worry about. It's just that they haven't had enough time to get to know each other properly yet, despite all Bridget's fondness for him. Let's face it, he can't offer her much company while he's a cripple. But then it's common knowledge that broken bones don't take long to heal. Maybe, once he's back on his feet, he'll be whisking her off all over town."

His eyebrows flickered briefly; he was wondering what Bridget had seen in this lame guy in the first place. She was bright and astute concerning the men she dated, and did not waste time on lost causes.

Chris knew Paula's intuition in this family was faultless and now that she had put his mind at rest, he went off to finish his chores, before relaxing in his usual chair. He wondered if he could give Bridget some treat to perk her up. Of course, he would check the theatre listings and take her to a London show soon. She would appreciate that. Obviously, what she would appreciate more would be for this guy to get his act together. Not that he would dare say that to Bridget at this stage.

And what about this Matt who Bridget had met?

A few months earlier, Matt had been a reluctant passenger in his brother Mike's car on a trip to a garden centre. He had peered out through the car window into the saturated landscape, regretting that his brother had persuaded him to come out in this terrible weather. The rain beat incessantly on the metal roof and against the glass and the windscreen wipers flicked monotonously to and fro on intermittent wipe, adding to his boredom. So much for Mike's idea that he needed some fresh air. How on earth could sitting in a car in the rain be good for his health? He would have preferred to stay in the cosy warmth of his armchair at his parents' home.

He should not be so ungrateful. The lengthy surgery had saved his lower leg, but self-pity often hit him despite all the efforts of his family. He had not shaken off those dark places completely. He pulled his jacket tighter around him and snuggled deeper into his turned-up collar. "Oh, come on Mike, will you!" he muttered, sighing impatiently. Why was he taking so long?

He gazed absently through the misting window at the cars arriving and departing from the almost empty car park. No wonder it was so deserted. Who in their right mind would plod around a plant nursery in this? Only insane people and idiots like Mike, he concluded.

Footsteps sounded on the gravel close by his door and leaves brushed against his side window. The plant to which the leaves belonged tapped and shook as it was juggled from one arm to the other by the person who was carrying it, who had halted in between the cars. Obviously unwilling to put the shrub down in the puddles filling the parking bays, the small figure was struggling to balance the shrub whilst rummaging for car keys.

Hampered as he was by having his leg in plaster, Matt wound down the window, only to have to duck swiftly away from a branch from the shrub which was swinging threateningly in his direction.

"Er, excuse me. Would you like me to hold that for you?" he offered.

The dark hood tilted back and a charming female face framed by wisps of damp hair smiled up at him. The rain was trickling down her face and dripping onto her already drenched raincoat.

"Thank you so much!" she said.

Matt opened the car door and leaned forward. "Here, let me have it on my lap, before you drop it."

The young woman hesitated at the sight of the plaster cast. "Are you sure?"

He nodded, then reached out and simply took the plant from her arms.

"Thank you so much. This won't take a minute," she assured him, her hand diving into her coat again. Having found the keys she hurried to unlock the car boot and began pushing things around to make space for the plant until she was satisfied it would fit. Returning to retrieve the plant, she apologised for the inconvenience.

"I shouldn't have been so lazy. I should have left it in the trolley and brought it to the car," she said.

"And then got a great deal wetter by making two extra unnecessary journeys, to take the trolley back and then return."

She smiled at his attempted humour and then pointed to her shoes, which were so damp the leather had darkened around the toes and heels. "It's a shame I didn't think of bringing wellingtons, either."

"You had better get out of the rain. Who's the plant for?"

"Thanks again. It's a present for my sister, I'm staying with her for a while."

"Nearby?"

She shook her head. Quickly turning back to the rear of the car, she placed the pot inside, pressed the boot shut and made for the driver's door. There she stopped briefly and beamed at him before, eager to get out of the downpour, she swiftly disappeared inside the vehicle. The car started immediately, and she was gone.

Matt stared after her and let out a long controlled breath. Those few minutes had been so refreshing. To talk to someone new, someone normal and friendly, a perfect stranger who was willing to chat, even for short time, made him miss the way he used to be.

The shape of a burly man splashed across the yard. He yanked open the driver's door and leapt inside, showering raindrops all over Matt. "Who was that then?" he asked, ignoring his brother's complaints.

"What kept you so long, Mike?" said Matt, ignoring the question.

"I was waiting for the rain to ease off, but I gave up. Anyway, I didn't want to interrupt your conversation with that attractive young woman," he added mischievously.

Matt grunted. He knew his brother was trying to rekindle his flagging ego, but he wasn't prepared to kid himself any more. His world had changed. It was difficult to pretend everything would be the same again.

"Yeah, yeah. OK, just drive me home." Matt muttered.

Silence filled the car as they headed back to the farm.

This trip out hadn't been the tonic Mike had intended. That brief moment of normality had come and gone so quickly that it left Matt a little more deflated. The glimpse of the pretty girl in the rain was only a reminder of how far he still had to go, physically and mentally.

Miles away and a little later, the unknown female Matt had just met had arrived at her sister's home. Delayed by the weather, Bridget knew Paula would have been looking out of the window every five minutes while Ray, her husband, would be gently trying to calm her down.

"Paula, she won't get here any quicker. At least it's stopped raining," he said. The curtains moved behind him again.

Indeed, Ray was grabbing the opportunity to sit in his

favourite chair, aiming for a last chance of peace for a while. But just then he heard a car draw up outside, and his wife dashed across the room to burst out of the front door so fast that it crashed back against the wall. More decorating, he noted with a forgiving little shake of the head, then, shrugging philosophically, he padded along behind to complete the welcome committee.

"Bridget, thank goodness!" Paula exclaimed the moment Bridget stepped out of the car, smiling.

Bridget's apology for being late was lost in the exchange of the alternating hugs with Paula and Ray. Their family affection for each other was bursting over. Anyone would think they had not seen each other for ages, instead of it being a regular visit.

The hugs and cuddles over, Bridget went to the boot of the car to fling it open.

"I had to stop off to get you this. Here, what do you think?" she asked with a smile of satisfaction. Exclamations of delight followed.

"Oh Ray, just look what she'as bought me!"

"Very nice, dear," he muttered. Plants and gardening were not his speciality, and taking the rest of the bags from the boot, he headed for the house.

The sisterly banter continued as Bridget followed Paula into the kitchen, where Bridget sighed appreciatively at how their comforting family dwelling simply gathered and wrapped people into its midst. She adored coming here, even when her chaotic young nephews filled it full of energy and noise.

"It's a wonder they haven't heard the rustle of bags already," she said. Then, as if at some invisible signal, mayhem burst out as the youngsters appeared, excited and full of questions. Bridget could only wonder what was in store for her.

Days later, Matt returned to the family farm after another hospital appointment. He had been thankful for these weeks staying with his supportive parents. Here in these familiar surroundings he could recuperate. Here he had escaped from the real world.

Anything was preferable to being alone in that big, empty London flat, where he had struggled to overcome his increasingly despondent mood, where too much silence and too much time found him continually churning over the accident. At home his parents had fussed over him and spoiled him for a while to begin with, but after that they had refused to let him wallow in those dark periods of useless reflection, however bad he felt. They made sure he had plenty to do and followed all the recommendations and suggestions in the consultant's latest assessment. At least the new routine of exercises gave him something to concentrate his mind on.

The morning had begun the same; as usual after breakfast, Matt had set off to the village, to potter about and chat to any locals he met. He felt safe in his own community.

Apart from the exercise, it made him socialise with other people, which he knew was important. He could not hide away forever.

After a cheerful word with the shop owner, he started on his return route, the slow rhythm of his feet and the tapping crutches sounding alternately along the pavement. He struggled on for a while, but the steps gradually got slower and slower; his legs were aching. It was stupid to push himself any further, he had to find somewhere to sit down. *Damn…*

The bench across the road on the small green was the nearest place to rest, and letting out an exasperated grunt, he thumped himself down on the wooden seat. Suddenly all his energy drained away and he slumped forward, burying his head in his hands, hoping there was no one else around. The last thing he wanted was to be noticed. Moments like this soon passed, and he desperately did not want anyone to make a fuss.

He gradually pulled himself together and sat back, thankful he had been left in peace. If that was the only setback he had to contend with today, he could count himself lucky.

"Hello again," came a soft voice, suddenly and a little apprehensively, from somewhere behind his shoulder.

He hadn't heard anyone approaching on the soft grass. Feeling himself tense up, he turned towards the sound, expecting to see a concerned local. Instead, the person who was standing there totally surprised him. It was the girl he had spoken to in the car park last weekend. How on earth? To see her here of all places, and it amazed him that she had recognised him after their one meeting and in bad light at that. Although the leg in plaster would have been a good indication, he realised.

"Oh, hello!" he finally managed.

"I wasn't sure it was you at first," she confessed. "I wasn't sure you would remember me. I was somewhat smothered in my waterproof when we met before."

He tactfully resisted admitting he remembered her simply because she had been the only new face he had seen in ages. His social skills were rusty, but he wanted to do his best to keep the conversation going.

"What brings you here? The village is well off the main road," he said.

She explained that she had come with her sister Paula to watch the swimming competition, because her children were in the school team competing against the local school. Matt remembered the packed car park at his old school on his way here. He should have realised something was happening, but he hadn't given it much thought.

"So why aren't you in there cheering them on?" he asked.

"I had just slipped out for some peace and quiet. I hadn't realised the amount of noise the children could make, all screaming encouragement to each other. It's enough to give anyone a headache." She sighed expressively.

Matt grinned sympathetically; he fully understood, remembering the deafening ruckus of the local children's sports days of the past. He had often taken part in encouraging them, himself. Yet it seemed like a lifetime ago.

"They won't miss you?" he enquired.

"Goodness, no. Much as I adore my nephews, they can be quite exhausting. Luckily the final races aren't scheduled for another hour. It gives me time to stretch my legs and get a sandwich from the local shop."

Just then a truck trundled by and tooted its horn twice in quick succession as it passed, making them both turn. Matt waved. "That's my Uncle Jim," he said.

"You're a local boy then? You live around here?"

"I used to. That's the only disadvantage of being a small-town boy, everyone knows everything about me. You know, the usual childhood pranks and mischief."

"Your less than perfect past, then," she joked.

He nodded, but was suddenly tongue-tied. But before the pause became too awkward, she asked him if he would also like a sandwich. She had been on her way to the store on the corner. He refused politely, and then regretted it. It would have been the perfect excuse for her to come back to join him on the green. He *was* out of practice! He was an idiot. He really did not want her to go so quickly. He liked talking to her, but all he could do was watch as she hurried off across the road. But as he sat there, annoyed at his lack of forethought, she miraculously returned and sat down on the bench beside him, as if there had never been any doubt that she would do exactly that.

Matt watched with a little surge of pleasure as she eagerly

unwrapped her sandwich and began munching it with gusto. Her ensuing cheerful chatter was refreshing to listen to. She told him in between the mouthfuls that she liked staying with her sister and her family in Kent. Normally she worked in the city, where she loved going to the theatres and shows.

"Gosh, that was good. Are you sure you don't want a sandwich? There's one left."

"Next time, maybe."

"Next time?" She grinned mischievously.

"Well – I mean if we bump into each other again."

Just what was the prospect of that? He doubted he would ever see her again. Unless – he hesitated. Should he?

"I have to come up to town, quite soon," he said. "I don't suppose… I could buy you a sandwich?"

She laughed. "A sandwich! That is different."

This was only the second time they had spoken to each other. Why should she agree? His injury would surely put her off. He shrugged, already prepared for a rejection as she delved into her bag instead of answering. Rather than consider his suggestion, she was deliberately turning her attention elsewhere.

"No, I just thought… if you had any free time," he mumbled dejectedly.

"Actually, that sounds quite nice," she said, glancing up briefly from her search.

He could not believe he had heard right. What was the probability of that? Then he saw she had found a pen and was scribbling on a piece of paper. She handed it to him.

"Here's my phone number. I can get quite busy, I don't work normal hours, but you can leave a message if I am out."

"Thanks," Matt clasped it firmly in his hand.

"Well, time is getting on – I'd better get back."

"I'll be in touch then," he added, no doubt too brightly.

"Yes – bye."

"Bye... Wait! I don't know your name."

"It's Bridget." She laughed, "What's yours?"

"It's Matt."

"Bye Matt. I hope to hear from you soon."

Still in shock, Matt watched her walk away and then wave back at him. How had that just happened? He had never expected for it to be that easy. He could not believe she was willing to risk going out with him. It had been ages since he had done anything actually normal.

Still a little jet-lagged, Chris dragged himself into work the next day and was surprisingly on time, despite the crowded tube, which made a change. Here back in the hub of Fleet Street, there would be a pile of assignments to catch up on and a list of important matters needing his attention immediately.

The office was its usual hustle and bustle, full of noise and people rushing about. Yet he had hardly exchanged the brief obligatory acknowledgements and the odd banter with other colleagues in the building than he was off to tackle Gerry, the Editor in Chief. After being told of the unwelcome attempt to have a junior reporter foisted on their office, Chris knew he had to prevent that happening.

This was a great start to the week. As one of the senior reporters on that floor, he had to apply some pressure to get this rectified. He did not stand on ceremony; he walked straight into Gerry's office and gave him a hard stare.

"Gerry, are you mad? We're a well-run team, the best you have. Why change it?" he said.

"Because he would learn more in your room."

Did he really think such cheap flattery would work? Chris did not back down or waver in his determination. He narrowed his eyes and tightened his jaw. He would stay there all day until the decision was changed.

Chris won the argument. The youngster was put next door, allowing both Cherry and Alan to breathe a sigh of relief. After which, he settled down for two hours of computer bashing before stopping for a well-deserved break to stretch his tight shoulder muscles. His colleagues did the same. The three of them had worked together for years, and a long-term friendship had developed. They met up socially and shared their opinions on everything.

Fetching a sandwich and a drink from the canteen, he leaned back in his chair.

"So how was the holiday then?" Alan asked.

"You caught the sun. You're looking good," Cherry chipped in.

"It was great. I feel much better for it. Glorious, great weather, warm sun and blue seas."

"Come on then, tell us what you got up to."

Not much, it was just his usual quiet beach holiday, he told them. A little sight-seeing, nothing special. He told them he had mastered the mountain bike, which surprised them both, although he didn't know when he would ride one again.

"No bruises or injuries then? How many times did you fall off?" said Cherry.

"I'm still in one piece, as you can see."

"Did the rest of the population survive?" she joked.

Chris had to think about his reply. Should he mention the one local he had nearly run over? It was not important, but having already told Bridget about it, he might be wise to share it with them as well. He did not need an inquisition later into why he hadn't. He repeated the same selective story he had told Bridget about his encounter with a local that had ended with her in a hedge, making it sound as amusing as he could. He brushed the incident off as casually as he could.

Alan laughed before slowly returning to his desk, while Cherry pulled a face at his stupidity. If she was sceptical about this mundane account, she did not openly query it. Chris gave her one of his rueful glances before clicking the computer back on. He had no intention of elaborating. His trivial encounters were insignificant and a stranger's apparent liaison with the older man was too sordid and too petty to mention. And not funny at all, the more he thought about it.

He let out a long sigh, acknowledging that all too soon his holiday would soon be a distant memory and within a few days everything would be back to normal. Cherry and Alan's interest in his summer break would fade as the deadlines came and went.

Of course there were always the last-minute changes to deadlines and the scheduled assignments, plus the weekly meeting with the editor to analyse the content of the news items. They were kept on their toes, And he did not mind melting back into the routine.

That evening he checked the wall calendar to see when he was meeting up with his old friends Tom Smith from the Working Men's Club and Mal Rhodes, his local postman. They had originally met when they had signed up at the further education centre for something different to do. Woodwork, well that was a joke. They had attended the library lectures thinking it would be interesting, only to find that they knew more about the subject than the speaker. They gave up on the self-improvement angle and settled for doing anything that would involve a lot of laughter at each other's expense.

The odd hobby came and went, including the time when the home-brewing kit stored in Mal's garage had exploded. Never to be tried again. The pitch and putt had been a good choice and the infrequent knockabout at the council-run tennis court had resulted in a couple of hours of light-hearted fun. As often as not they were content for merely a social evening out. Another week to go. He put a big red circle around the date, so as not to forget.

Chris was definitely back in work mode. He had attended a press launch for a major construction project with most of the other media. The meeting had been full of arguments, accusations and awkward questions from the audience. The developers were being stumped by the technical claims of their opponents. It was a lengthy and noisy event, with the result that Chris was running late. Back at the office, he had been unable to make sense of the voice recorder because of the number of overlapping opinions drowning each other out. He pulled a face. He would have to rely on his notes and his memory, which meant working late again.

Cherry passed him on his way in, as she was leaving. "Don't forget to remind Bridget I expect her on Saturday," she said. She wanted no excuses; she expected them both. To be honest, he had half-forgotten about the invitation. He had also not followed up the idea of taking Bridget to a London show. He had better do that now. He rang the twenty-four hour theatre booking office, only to find everything was fully booked for months. It was still the holiday season and tourist companies always booked in bulk for their clients. Common sense should have told him that when he first thought of the idea, he scolded himself.

He frowned at the empty office and checked the time to make sure it was not too late to phone his sister. Yes, she should still be up. But when Bridget answered, he could tell that she was still not her usual bubbly self. He gabbled on as if he had not noticed, saying he hoped she had remembered about coming to Cherry's shindig with him on Saturday. It was always an enjoyable evening and she knew most of the crowd that would be there. Cherry would be hurt if she did not go, he added. A little emotional blackmail should make sure she attended.

The usual merry atmosphere lit up the old houseboat in Putney as the evening progressed. The boat was a converted Dutch barge with a large deck, the interior a mass of coloured Bohemian and folk art and crowded with European memorabilia. Cluttered and definitely a little old fashioned, it had its normal welcoming vibe. These gatherings were known for a mix of different nationalities and cultures from the local area. A few old hippies and beatniks were there, some of them in flamboyant outfits, while Cherry in contrast flaunted herself in a thin strap top and patterned cotton floating skirt. Ethnic food from many cultures was on offer and live music from a variety of musicians provided the most diverse atmosphere you could hope to find anywhere.

He liked Cherry; she was a good friend. He knew she had rebelled against her well-educated and privileged background of expensive private schools and finishing schools abroad to become another thankless, hard-working hack. She thrived on it, and everyone knew her as the most down-to-earth person around; she had lived a simple life on this outlandish old hulk for years.

He had hoped that the lively evening would cheer Bridget up, but it did not seem to. Despite Cherry being the usual great hostess, and the jolly atmosphere which always engulfed the old houseboat, Bridget's lack of spark was evident. Although she smiled and returned some of the banter, Chris and Cherry could both see it was an effort. Despite all the merriment it was clear that Matt, with all his hang-ups, had got under her skin. Chris was glad that his love life had never been this fraught. Well, he didn't remember it being like that.

Over a drink he admitted to his colleague that he did not have any instant solutions to help his sister's mood. Slipping down to sit beside him on the step of the open doorway, Cherry confided that she did not believe there were any instant solutions; they did not exist. Life was not like that. There were no quick fixes when it came to emotions, she told him. He knew she was right.

Maybe a change of scene would help, Cherry suggested. Chris considered it and during the rest of the evening began to think of how he could get this to work. Time away would clear her head. On the way home he broached the idea to Bridget, hoping that by the time they reached her front door, she would agree.

"Look, how about us taking a trip one weekend? I was thinking we could go up to visit Aunt Mary soon. We haven't seen her for ages. You always love it up there. I'm sure I can wangle some time off."

Bridget did not look that keen, but Chris was in a persuasive mood, full of gentle but enthusiastic encouragement. There was no reason not to, he pleaded, determined to win her around. A little reluctantly, she promised to think about it. Well, Chris was not going to give her time to think about it, she would only find excuses. He knew her too well. Since she had not given him a definite, positive 'no' on the spot, he was going to act quickly. He would phone Aunt Mary in the morning. Once the arrangements were made, Bridget could hardly back out.

CHAPTER 3

Several weeks earlier, Matt had opened the front door of his luxury flat in London and tossed the keys into a dish while Mike shuffled past him through the hall to open some windows. The place needed a good airing, as no one had been in there for months.

Matt gazed about the place, familiarizing himself with the contents once more. There were things he had forgotten, the modern starkness, the large prints bought on a whim from a gallery, expensive rugs and the impractical glass table. Even the view overlooking the river failed to attract his attention any more, yet it was that and the location which had inspired him to buy it in the first place. It felt strange. This was not a home, while his brother's small flat, full of untidy clutter, had a warmth and cosiness that his place lacked. This had never been a proper home. He regretted it now.

The photos on the kitchen wall had a greater impact, the sudden unnecessary reminder of his too-recent past causing him to catch his breath inadvertently. He had forgotten they were there. He turned away, unwilling to look at them, and began checking the contents of the cupboards in an effort to ignore their effect on him. *Damn!*

"Sorry, I should have taken them down, said Mike from the doorway. "Maybe it was a mistake coming back here. Would you be better off staying at my place instead tonight?"

"I'll be fine. It's only for a couple of days. Where have you put everything else?"

"Locked away in a suitcase, in the spare room."

Satisfied, Matt began putting the groceries away. He could easily avoid the spare room altogether and the wardrobe full of expensive suits and shirts. Once the hospital appointments in London had finished, he intended to sell up. This large, impersonal showcase was no use to him now. It did not impress anyone.

The moment Mike had left, Matt sank into one of the ultra-comfortable chairs, intending to settle back into his cocoon and let the world go by without having to consider being part of it. He had been in low spirits. After finally plucking up the nerve yesterday to phone the telephone number Bridget had given him, there had been no answer. He had mumbled some garbled words into the answering machine and left his mobile number. He hated these machines. Yesterday and today had passed with no return call, and he began to assume that she was probably trying to find an excuse to let him down gently.

He had spent ages before making that call thinking about the best place to meet her. The prospect of finding a location suitable for them both seemed daunting. There were several issues to take into account. He did not know how well she knew London. It should be somewhere she could easily find and get to, with maybe a car park? If she was working, could she get time off? Now he was getting nervous. He would prefer somewhere quiet, in the fresh air and uncrowded, with seats, a pond and a café, places to rest if he was tired. Would she mind that?

So where could they safely meet? One of the London parks seemed the best choice, but which? He had to be careful. He did not want it too near his flat or anywhere he might bump into people who knew him, even casually by sight. He did not want this chance ruined before it had begun.

Richmond Park was large enough to get lost in, but he had often spent hours of training there to keep up his important top level of fitness, early in the mornings. No doubt his fellow health fanatics would probably still be pounding the same tracks. He did not want to risk it. Besides, it was a bit hilly, although the Pen ponds and the café near the car park had an advantage. Likewise, Wimbledon Common was ruled out; Queen's Mere pond was gloomy and surrounded by trees, and the Windmill tea rooms and windmill museum would attract visitors.

He settled for Bushy Park, near to Hampton Court. Yes the main car park would be too popular because of the Diana Fountain, but the next car park further in, had a walk around Heron Pond with the Pheasantry café even further away from the obvious attraction.

He had worked it all out, and now his hopeful expectations had been dashed. She was obviously not interested. There were moments when he hated being him.

A little later, he heard the phone ringing out behind him. No one knew he was back in town, so he waited for his own answering machine to kick in, to find out who it was. Except it didn't, because he remembered Mike had had the service provider remove the option soon after the accident, after it had been swamped with messages. Even one from Chloe, who had asked when he would be ready to party again. Insensitive bitch!

Then his mobile rang. The display showed a number he did not instantly recognise. "Hello," he answered, a little defensively, unsure who he would have to talk to.

"Hello Matt, this is Bridget. I'm sorry I missed you. I've been away sourcing materials for our next client. It's been a bit hectic. It was quite late when I got home yesterday, so I didn't check my messages until today."

It sounded plausible, and her voice was as bright as he remembered.

"You said you were coming up to town," she went on. "Do you know when?"

"I'm here already. I'll be here for a few days. I – are you – will you be..."

His voice died on him and he could hear her snigger, not unkindly, at the other end. Even if he only had her company for a short while, it would be more than he had hoped for.

"Are you trying to suggest we actually meet up for this sandwich?" she asked sympathetically.

"Hmm... well. Yes and very badly it seems."

She told him she had some free time tomorrow, if that was convenient. He leapt at the opportunity, quickly suggesting Bushy Park in the morning, because it would not be too crowded at that time of day.

"I don't want to be knocked off my feet before I'm back on them properly," he joked. She agreed and suggested they could feed the ducks on the pond, and perhaps even get some pastries at the café afterwards, if he fancied it.

"Not too boring for a country boy?" she teased.

"Not for this one." He managed to laugh.

Mike had only agreed to give his brother a lift to the car park at this hour to satisfy his growing curiosity, because Matt was being deliberately mysterious.

"Bushy Park? Why there?"

"I'm going for a walk," Matt told him as casually as he could manage.

Walk? Mike pondered silently. Since when had Matt ever dragged himself there for a walk?

A few minutes after they got there another car drew up

beside them, and Mike had his answer. Bridget stepped out and waved at Matt, and Matt quickly started struggling out of the car to join her. His brother grabbed his sleeve.

"Hang on. What have I missed?" Mike demanded. "How did you manage that?"

Matt hadn't a clue, and he didn't care. He finally yanked himself free and was out of the car, without explaining anything. Nothing was going to spoil this morning. There was nothing wrong with kidding himself that this was a how a normal day should be.

"I brought some bread for the ducks," Matt said to her, grinning and waving a bag in his hand.

"So did I," she admitted, waving a similar bag.

"I had to buy some," he confessed as they began to walk.

"Likewise. What a pair of idiots we are."

They both laughed as they made their way along the path to the pond, Bridget taking slow steps in time with the pattern of his movements and Matt smiling at everything around him. The ducks had gathered at the side of the pond, quacking noisily, scrambling and flapping their wings for the best place, while other birds were gathering at a distance and heading for them.

"Look out! I think we had better feed them quickly, before we get attacked," she said.

Balancing against one crutch, Matt stood beside her as they threw pieces of bread into the water at regular intervals, tossing pieces further out to those birds which were squawking at the rear.

"You look like Long John Silver like that," she gently teased.

He did not mind her comments at all; he was glad that she felt relaxed enough to treat him normally.

"Pieces of eight, pieces of eight!" he squawked suddenly, giving his best impression of Long John's parrot in *Treasure Island*.

"Hopeless. Utterly hopeless." She giggled.

He nodded, pulled a silly face and shrugged. "Obviously I have no acting talent," he sighed.

"There is nothing either good or bad, but thinking makes it so."

"Where did that come from?"

"Shakespeare of course."

He was surprised.

"Do you know how long your leg will take to mend?" She could not help asking him that.

"No, not really," he replied, without trying to hide the disappointment in his voice.

Bridget sensed his reluctance to talk about it and turned her attention back to the paper bag. She tipped it upside down over the water, emptying the last of the crumbs to the splashing, squabbling ducks. After which she scrunched up the bag into a small ball, a little sad that it had all gone. Matt scrunched up his own bag, then took hers from her. Taking careful aim, he lined up the target on the far side of the path and successfully tossed them both into the rubbish bin. After that he punched the air with his fist, pleased at his mundane success.

"You promised me a sandwich," she said.

"So I did."

They made their way to the café, where their conversation was light, casual and even silly. The time raced by and eventually they walked back towards the car park.

"So, when are you back in town? Where do you have in mind for our next outing?"

Her comment stopped him in his tracks. He looked at her smile. He could see she meant it. Matt had never considered that there might be a next time. He hadn't thought that far ahead. He was still thinking himself lucky to have had her company for today.

"You want to put up with me again?" he said.

"You're not that bad," she smirked, as she unlocked her car door.

Matt was amazed.

Matt hardly heard any of the third-degree examination from Mike, which continued all the way to the hospital. The routine X-rays confirmed that the bones were healing in alignment. With metal screws and plates holding the bones in place, it should have been an automatic conclusion, but the complication of separated fragments and torn ligaments had caused problems. Normally he hated the check-ups, the clinical smell and the memories. Today he had forgotten all of those things; today he was thinking how he had enjoyed those earlier quiet hours, the two of them strolling along together. He had forgotten such simple pleasures. He really hoped she would not tire of him too soon.

Meanwhile, back at her little terraced house, Bridget was gazing out of the window, staring absently into space and wondering why she liked Matt. What was it that had made her give him her number that day without any hesitation, without even thinking, something she had never, ever done before? And why she had no doubts about meeting him again? There was something about his vulnerability, his tired smile and his unkempt hair.

Bridget had confided in Paula first and then Chris later that she was seeing someone new and how she had first met Matt in the pouring rain. She confessed, rather shyly, that she liked him a lot. They had both been pleased for her, although when she told them that Matt was injured and on crutches, her brother-in-law Ray had jokingly asked why she had not picked someone who was still in one piece. Typical Ray!

It was amazing how easily their tentative casual arrangement continued. It felt quite intriguing. Neither of them felt the need to impress the other. She had even told him that she thought he would look much more handsome without the stubble and short beard. Her kind opinion came naturally; she did not even think she needed to be tactful. Having always been used to teasing her brother Chris about his appearance, she considered Matt similar fair game.

Matt did not take offence; he just grinned. How was

she to know that he did not want to look handsome? That untidy growth protected him from being what he had been before. He was enthralled by her easy banter as she gradually told him more about herself, claiming to be an ordinary working girl.

"No one is ordinary in this life," he claimed.

She went on to mention her sister and her brother Chris, including the fact that he had just gone off to Sardinia after borrowing one of her suitcases. Then she sniggered and nudged him affectionately, before apologising for rambling on too much.

Matt had enjoyed learning more and more about her, while in contrast he had been quite reticent about relating his own potted history. She was however slowly dragging things out of him that he did not want to talk about. How could he prevent her asking more and more difficult questions? One of them was about the type of accident he had had. What could he tell her?

"I was knocked down in a car park," he told her flatly.

He could not believe he had actually said it. That had been a simple enough explanation, without being a lie. He had given her as little information as possible. He did not want to remember the truth nor the details of his injuries. He was winning the battle of putting that behind him. He had gambled on her sympathetic nature, hoping she would not pursue the matter, and it had worked.

That had passed by without too much difficulty, and his deliberate evasiveness continued to be enough. He had waffled about his earlier employment; the farm work, the deliveries to London markets, the canning factory and as a labourer on building sites in the city. Nor did he want to put her off by divulging the lifestyle he had revelled in before his accident. Headstrong and wayward, he had been determined to enjoy himself. He had learnt his lesson. There was nothing to be proud of. Night clubs and wine bars were a thing of the past.

He longed to be back to normal, longed to be able to take Bridget out properly, longed to go to the cinema rather than watch films on the television. He just had to be patient. A patient being patient, that was a joke. It wasn't in his nature.

It had been the last meeting with Bridget, just before Chris returned from holiday, which had caused the problem for Matt.

Mike had sympathetically done his best to stay in the background, something which was increasingly difficult, especially when he was the one ferrying Matt around most of the time.

She cheerfully greeted him as normal when he arrived that afternoon. "Hello Mike."

"Ah, my brother, my chauffeur and minder," Matt quipped.

"Minder?" Bridget was puzzled by his choice of word.

Hell! That was the first mistake Matt had made for a long time. Luckily Mike was quick to cover up the blunder. He gave Matt a playful clip round the ear. "It's a poor joke.

I'm in the police force. Part of the Metropolitan Police, in London," he told her. So, the slip-up had passed unnoticed.

"Serious stuff then," Bridget beamed, obviously impressed.

Matt nodded. He was quite proud of his brother.

"So, what about your family? What does your brother do for a living?" Mike asked.

"Chris? Oh, he's a newspaper reporter. He loves chasing stories and doing interviews."

Matt felt himself stiffen. He shot a horrified glance towards his brother, who wasn't looking his way. Not that Bridget noticed any of this as she merrily chatted on. Suddenly Matt was stuck for words. Panic raced around his mind as he tried to remember what he had innocently told her. The last thing he wanted was some damned reporter delving into his life. He did not know how to handle this bombshell. He needed to think. What could he do?

Matt interrupted the conversation, holding his leg and complaining he felt tired. Mike looked at his brother, suspecting that that might not be exactly true. But he went along with it, quickly offering to drive him home.

"What was all that about?" Mike questioned suspiciously the moment they were in the car.

"Her brother works for the *Despatch!*"

"So? Matt, calm down. There is nothing to worry about."

"I may have been in the news, but I don't want it resurrected. You know what they're like."

Matt was in a state. His mind was racing. How could this happen?

On the Sunday morning after Cherry's party on her old house boat, Chris phoned their Aunt Mary in Cambridge before Bridget could change her mind. Their aunt was excited, gushing with delight at the idea. Of course, they could come to stay any time, she was always pleased to see them. Her own children, Callum and Rosie, were home for the summer, from university and college respectively. It would be great for them all to catch up. The four of them had always got on well together despite their age differences, and the house would be just like old times with the four of them here again.

The journey up to Cambridge saw a remarkable difference in Bridget. The further north they travelled, the more calm and relaxed she seemed to be. She did not refer to Matt once, and nor did Chris. He had high hopes for this trip. Within a couple of hours a noisy reunion was in full swing, all of them talking at once.

The family bond renewed, the four of them spent the first day in Cambridge, soaking up the atmosphere of the old university town. They roamed The Banks, viewing the various colleges and watching the punts on the river. Then from Midsummer Common, opposite the University Boat House, they had a picnic, while the rowing crews trained on the Cam in front of them. They were a sight to be admired, although not envied, Chris thought. All those tired aching muscles at the end of the day was not his idea of enjoyment.

Their aunt smiled at the band of young people as they set off the next day without having made any plans. They were quite content to explore the countryside and villages, and stop when they spotted something interesting. Somehow, they found themselves at Marsham, where Aston Hall and its estate were now open to the public after years of being in private ownership. Bridget and Chris had never seen the place before and were quite keen to find out what it was like. They were sure their cousins had not been there either.

"What do you think? Shall we go?" said Bridget. They were pleased that no one voiced any objection. Rosie did not voice an opinion – she obviously did not care either way – while Callum simply shrugged and seemed less than impressed, but said nothing. It was decided then, Chris confirmed; Aston Hall it was.

Callum fidgeted about in the front seat and coughed rather oddly in an effort to draw his attention. Chris raised his eyebrows and frowned a silent question, but his cousin only stared back, wide-eyed and frowning, as if he expected Chris to read his mind. Which he could not. Chris ignored him and turned his attention back to driving, following the road signs.

Aston Hall was easy to find and Chris headed for the ticket booth, paid the entrance money, and took a few maps and booklets. Returning to the car, he could see the girls were already standing waiting, yet Callum's sullen face and odd glances at Rosie threatened to put a dampener on the day. Chris wasn't going to allow that. Luckily the girls had wandered off together arm in arm, with Bridget chatting away to her cousin, leaving the men to their own devices.

The men dawdled behind, which suited Chris, because he was going to take photos of the gardens for Paula as he explored. Callum was trudging silently at his heels as Chris checked his camera. It was peaceful, quiet and not busy. Yet the moment the girls had turned the corner, his cousin grabbed his sleeve and hauled him aside, out of sight of other people.

"You bloody idiot! How insensitive can you be?" he snapped.

Chris looked blankly at him, shaking himself free.

"Don't tell me you don't know."

"Know what?" Chris demanded.

"That this was Rosie's childhood home before her parents died! It might upset her to be back here. She might not want to be reminded of that time. Didn't you notice how quiet she was?" He was almost spitting the words out.

Chris glared back. This was news to him. It would be to Bridget as well.

"But she didn't object to coming here. She had every chance to say no."

"Maybe she was being polite," his cousin growled.

"Hold on there, Callum. Rosie didn't seem upset when she went off with Bridget, from what I could see. Besides, has anyone ever asked her if she wanted to come back to see the place?"

Callum shook his head.

"Then maybe someone should have! She seems fine being here," Chris declared firmly, ending the confrontation.

Callum stomped off. Chris let him go; he did not mind wandering around the place on his own. The whole estate was a total delight, and there was so much to see. Formal gardens, herb gardens, small walled areas, vast open spaces, meadows and orchards beyond. He sat on the bench and unwrapped a chocolate bar, thinking how lucky Rosie had been to grow up here. It must have been wonderful to have all this space to explore. He could not believe all her memories would be bad.

When he found Bridget on her own in the café while Rosie went to buy postcards, he quickly asked her how the visit had gone. Bridget seemed a little puzzled by such a question.

"Why?"

"Callum was concerned that she might have been upset at coming back here, because this is where she and her parents lived, when she was a child. before they died."

Bridget paused, checking they were still alone.

"Well, that would explain a lot. Her behaviour in the car was out of character when you first suggested coming here. She looked quite pensive and went silent, then she chewed her lip and clenched her hands together. I had to ask her if she was feeling all right. Although she nodded, I almost told you to turn around, but she stopped me. Once we arrived at the entrance, she seemed to relax. Her eyes were darting all over the place. And as we started walking around the gardens, she brightened up completely, there was no stopping her, she was keen to explore every nook and cranny. If you're right about her spending her childhood here, then she was clearly happy with the memories she had. I think she actually loves his place," said Bridget.

"I do," Rosie whispered over their shoulders, making them turn.

Rosie had returned with her purchases and proudly laid them out on the table top for them to admire.

"I didn't know if I wanted to see the place again. I didn't know how I would feel being here. I was worried it would have changed too much – but I am pleased it hasn't."

She wrinkled her nose and smiled with genuine pleasure.

A relieved Chris slowly finished his cup of coffee, thankful that he hadn't responsible for upsetting Rosie. He would have hated to have done that.

The conversation during the drive back was casual and amicable. Rosie chatted on about her friends and what they were doing over the holidays, while Callum, having got over his sulk, was telling them about his life at university. It concluded with Rosie finally putting the whole afternoon into perspective.

"Thank you for today. I admit I was apprehensive at first about coming. But once I was here in the beautiful gardens, I realised it meant a great deal. I could touch the past without being overwhelmed with any lingering sadness. It was wonderful. I needed to go back. I should have done it years ago," Rosie sighed.

Bridget and Chris exchanged satisfied glances. Callum need not have worried. Rosie had dealt with those sensitive issues in her own way and come through apparently unscathed. Chris had to admit, she was a remarkable young woman.

They arrived back at the house happy and tired, and looking forward to enjoying the scrumptious meal their aunt would have prepared for them. Rosie went dancing into the sitting room to tell their aunt where they had been, the postcards in her hand. Yet Aunt Mary seemed hesitant to look at them. Was it only Chris and Bridget who noticed the slight awkwardness? Chris frowned thoughtfully and Bridget widened her eyes as their aunt disappeared into the kitchen to check on the food. Rosie was still engrossed in her postcards and Callum had gone to switch the television on.

"What do you make of that?" Bridget whispered. Chris was not sure. Bridget, having the same curious nature as her brother, was now completely enthralled and wanted to find out more. No one had told them much about Rosie's history or the full circumstances behind her being taken in by their widowed aunt. Bridget confided that she meant to have a private talk with Aunt Mary later that night and meant to have the mystery solved by the time they went back to London.

"Are you sure you should?"

The expression on Bridget's face gave him the answer.

"Be diplomatic," he warned.

Chris was quite willing to let her try, and was not surprised when she bustled everyone else out of the way to help her aunt clear up in the kitchen. The two women soon settled into a quiet, confidential conversation. It was obvious that they would be talking for ages, long after the rest of them had gone to bed.

The weekend over, they made much of their goodbyes, hugging and kissing everyone several times and promising to visit more often. They had only gone a few miles before Bridget, unable to wait, started relating the details of the conversation last night.

"There is so much to tell you," she said.

Chris could not concentrate on listening to her properly and driving at the same time. "Later. Tell me when we stop for coffee," he grunted, braking defensively in response to some idiot driver ahead.

Ignoring him, Bridget began to explain how Aunt Mary had been alarmed by their venture to Aston Hall, considering it thoughtless of them. But since they had not known of its significance, she had forgiven them. Aunt Mary had said that she was relieved and pleasantly surprised by Rosie's apparent unconcern at going back there.

"At least we didn't end up in her bad books over an

innocent mistake," said Chris.

They pulled into Birchanger Services, bought a coffee and found a quiet spot to sit.

"Come on then, let's hear it all," said Chris as he sipped his drink.

Bridget had plenty to tell him. Apparently, Rosie's father had been one of the groundsmen for the estate and they had lived in one of the cottages in the grounds. Aunt Mary had been best friends with Rosie's parents for a long time, which was why she had so eagerly adopted Rosie after their death in a car crash.

"We have always known Rosie was adopted. It's no big thing," said Chris.

"Aunt Mary also told me about the day she had brought Rosie home to live with them, wrapped in a blanket, after being uprooted from everything she knew," Bridget went on. "She sat cradling her in her arms. Rosie was terribly shy and stubbornly silent, although they did everything they could to make her welcome. Her belongings were put in the spare room, which was specially decorated for her, and the box containing all her toys was left open, for her to place them wherever she wanted, but they stayed undisturbed in the box. She never touched them. They are now stored in the attic. That is so sad."

Chris would have agreed it was sad, if he had had the chance, but Bridget was in full flow.

"She told me how kind Callum was to Rosie. He offered Rosie his own scruffy bear since she would not touch her own toys. He was only six, a year older than Rosie. Don't you think that was touching? From that first tentative gesture, their friendship developed into a bond of unspoken loyalty. It's no wonder he is so protective."

"Yes, yes. It was very sweet."

He had switched off, his attention elsewhere. For goodness' sake, how long was this going to take?

Chris let out a deep breath and checked his watch. He was mindful of the traffic getting back into London. He had promised to be back at work after lunch. It was no good, he had to take the matter in hand.

"Bridget, I'm going to be late," he said firmly, standing up and walking away.

"I thought you would be more interested," Bridget complained as she plonked herself back in the car.

"Why? Rosie has grown up into a perfectly well-adjusted young lady."

Rosie was Rosie. He accepted things as they were, while his sister screwed up her face and glared through the windscreen. Her silence was deafening. Chris relented slightly.

"There's no need to sulk. You did well to coax Aunt Mary into speaking about it. I'm sure she was glad of a sympathetic ear after all this time."

"Yes, you're right," she admitted fondly.

Chris smiled to himself. He considered that the weekend had been a success as well as enlightening. His original plan had been to take Bridget's mind off of Matt for a while, and it looked like her new interest in young Rosie's prior history had definitely achieved that. He was certain that Bridget would be on the phone to Paula the moment she was home to tell her everything. She seemed to have forgotten the disappointment and minor difficulties concerning Matt.

On the last part of their journey home, Chris decided he would actually test his sister's attitude regarding Matt.

"When are you seeing Matt next?" Chris asked casually. All he knew was that they usually met on the days when his brother drove him up to town for hospital appointments.

She gave a deep sigh of resignation. "Who knows?"

Chris arrived back at work to find Alan's friends from the sports section clustered around his desk. Oblivious to his presence, they were talking about the chances of Chris Froome winning the coming Tour de France for the second time, together with their appreciation of the daily stages over the torturous mountain climbs. Chris cleared his throat extremely loudly, hoping to shift them, but then they began discussing Lewis Hamilton's victory in the British Grand Prix in June.

This was too much. Chris frowned. He stood by his desk, slapped his hand down noisily and glared at them. It was difficult enough to cover all their workload as it was without his friend being distracted by social chit chat in working hours. They had deadlines to meet. He was not pleased.

"Do you mind taking yourselves back to your own

office?" he said. "I have work to do. Even if you don't!"

They quickly scuttled off to their own offices, mumbling their apologies. Alan, head down, was shuffling the papers in front of him.

"For God's sake Alan, don't encourage them," said Chris. "You're late for your assignment."

Alan disappeared, leaving Chris to check what else was on the list. What was worth following up? Which would interest the public appetite more? There were rumblings about coal mines closing around the country, rumblings which could escalate into protests and other tensions. It was a very sensitive and political issue, and he would have to keep his eye on what was developing. Interviewing the protagonists was never pleasant. Decisions, decisions. He was not even going to follow up last month's protests about the BBC proposing job cuts to make savings. That was old news.

Then his grasshopper mind kicked in. Of course, the part of his work he enjoyed the most was doing occasional in-depth articles for a fortnightly glossy magazine. He loved the research and the people behind any story. He wondered what his editor had in mind for the next issue.

He looked at the list again, struggling to pick a subject he felt would be topical. He made a few phone calls. Then he picked up his voice recorder and notebook, shoved them in his pocket and headed out, leaving a note on Cherry's desk to let her know where he had gone.

CHAPTER 4

Once home, Bridget and Chris had returned to their work routine. Bridget was in better spirits these days. She breezed into Chris's house on the Friday evening as usual, smiling and light hearted.

"You're looking chipper," he said.

Bridget had often found herself thinking affectionately about Rosie. They had been talking together over the last few days and naturally she wanted to keep her brother up to date with what was going on. It appeared that Rosie was still pleased about her return to Aston Hall and could not wait to go again.

"Well, there's nothing stopping her now. She can go anytime she likes," Chris had pointed out.

Which was fine, except that Callum had wanted to

tag along, his sister told him. Apparently, Rosie had had to be quite firm with him. She did not want his company, preferring to go on her own.

Chris could see Rosie's point; no doubt she would prefer quiet private time to herself to mull over her precious childhood memories. Why would she want Callum, caring brother that he might be, tagging along, dogging her every footstep, full of questions? Of course she wouldn't.

"Would you want your brother tagging along?" he asked.

"No, not really." She giggled.

"There you go then."

When Bridget said she had been thinking, it was always a dangerous sign to Chris. He held his breath, unable to guess where this was going. Thankfully it was a suggestion to invite Rosie down to London for a show or shopping, some time in the future. He relaxed. There was nothing wrong with that.

Dare he ask about Matt? Was she going to mention him? But without prompting, she did, quite simply and philosophically. She told her brother she was not prepared to mope around after him any more. She wasn't going to put up with his daft behaviour. Matt had to sort himself out before they saw each other again, that was her ultimatum. This time she was laying down the rules. He would have to do better, and she was not going to make it easy for him.

In recent days Mike had endlessly tackled Matt about his

recent lack of contact with Bridget, dismissing all the lame excuses he was given.

"I could shake the living daylights out of you, Matt, you're being stupid. It's been a week. You must call her."

Matt shook his head. How could he? He didn't know what to say to her. He could hardly explain the reason for his foolish behaviour. The only thing he could do was keep it simple.

"I'm sorry," he said into the answering machine. He had to repeat it ten times before he had a reply. He grabbed the mobile, but her call was far less friendly than he had expected.

"Sorry for what? Sorry for being so unsociable? Sorry for making me think you were worth caring about? Sorry for making me miserable?" Bridget did not mince her words.

"Sorry for being such an idiot," Matt tried.

"Is that all?"

Matt knew he was in trouble.

"I miss you," he added hopefully.

Bridget did not reply; she had hung up.

Chris was putting together a longer feature for the magazine supplement. His piece was centred on the closure of the Marshall Theatre, which had been failing for too many years. Originally it had been packed every night, but like most things tastes had changed and audiences had declined, and now it stood empty and in some disrepair.

His editor required a fitting and suitable epitaph.

Chris had already researched the theatre's origins and the number of owners it had had through the years. There had been various permutations to its layout, but Chris knew the format he wanted to use. He intended to include any interesting reminiscences with the articles he already had on the theatre's heyday. He intended to chase up the names of the once-famous actors who had appeared there, to find out if they wanted to contribute any outstanding additional memories.

He was given the name of one former actor, Bill Stanley, who, it turned out, had many amusing stories and would be delighted to have Chris interview him. Stanley preferred to talk face to face, as conversations over the phone were not the same, he declared. Chris did not mind that at all; he had always felt that the personality and expressions of people gave more depth to any story. The only problem was that Chris would have to visit him at his home in Peterborough, since the old man, being an invalid, did not travel these days. Chris did not mind that either, since it got him out of the office for a decent time.

Then, remembering his promise to Aunt Mary that one of them would visit her soon, it occurred to him that since he would pass Cambridge on the way to Peterborough, he could to call in on the way back and maybe stay overnight. He just had to get it agreed with his editor.

Chris's assignment out of London went better than he had dared to hope. The old man was a mine of information and full of jolly, nostalgic tales. Chris could have listened to him for hours. Indeed, with a notebook and tape full of brilliant recollections, he had been quite sorry to leave.

Having left Peterborough, the traffic had been light and he found himself well ahead of time. He did not want to get to Aunt Mary's too early and on a whim, took a detour back to Aston Hall; He did not know why, but it suddenly seemed a good idea to look at the place again. When he arrived there were not many people about, either visitors or staff. He idly wondered if there was anyone still there who might have known Rosie's family, but he did not hold out much hope of that.

He still had not visited the main house, but he would do that another time. Not that it looked that special compared to the many other period historic mansions that he and his siblings had been dragged around with their grandmother as a child. There were few he had not visited.

Chris wandered the grounds and eventually found an old man working in the kitchen garden next to the empty stable block. Gently he began his enquiries by commenting on how well the place had been kept, to find his acquaintance quite amicable for conversation. Not many visitors were sociable enough to express their admiration or chat with the gardeners, the man remarked.

"Have you worked here long?" Chris asked.

The man nodded and Chris let him relate the changes he had seen through the years before attempting to put his other question.

"My name's Chris Page, by the way."

"George Watson. Pleased to meet you."

"I came here a while ago with my sister and cousins. One of them used to live on the estate when she was small. I don't suppose you would remember a little girl – Rosie, Rosie Tolhern?"

"Indeed I do!" Mr Watson exclaimed. His face lit up and his eyes crinkled with pleasure, as he stood there with memories obviously flooding back. "Goodness, she was such a sweet little child. How I miss her."

"She came to live with my Aunt Mary after her parents' accident."

"And is she well? Does she still draw?"

Draw? Chris was confused. As long as he could remember Rosie had never demonstrated any interest in drawing. He had never seen her with a pencil in her hand. He had never seen her attempting any childish scribbles or even having a colouring book. Unlike Bridget, who had been born with a pencil in her hand and littered the house with crayons, paints and sketchbooks. And woe betide anyone who dared to move them.

Chris confirmed she was fine, but admitted he had not known she drew.

"That's such a shame. I remember her filling page after page with pictures of this place – the cottage; the farm, the gardens, everything which had been part of her life here. The broken fence, the little copse at the bottom meadow, even the scarecrow. Her enthusiasm seemed endless."

"I have never seen any sketches. I expect she put them away in the attic, where she kept everything else from here," Chris responded.

"Ah well, I suppose it's no wonder. Poor lass, memories are not always kind ones."

George Watson was clearly assuming that Chris would know everything that had happened, but he did not. He could only offer a tentative smile, preferring not to betray the fact that he had no idea what the man was talking about.

"But I understood she was very happy here," he said.

"Oh, she was, but, well..."

The old man fell silent, clearly reluctant to continue, and Chris did not want to push the matter. He had already found out more than he had expected. The gardener slowly walked off to go back to his digging, while Chris remained seated watching him. The old man stuck the fork into the ground, then stopped, returned and put his tools down.

"That was such a sad time. No doubt she will be keeping her precious sketches safe. It will be hard to look at them after losing Jake and then her parents." It was as if he had been thinking of the reason for some time.

Jake? Who was Jake? Chris had never heard him mentioned before. He could only conclude that he must have been another child on the estate. He was about to ask when old man enlightened him further.

"She and Jake were inseparable. The pair of them were always running about the place, as happy as can be. They were no trouble at all. Of course, him dying changed everything."

What? Hardly had he got to grips with the introduction of this Jake when he was being told of his death. George Watson's voice faltered, his shoulders sagged and his face crumpled in sorrow. He stopped talking. Chris reached out to touch him, concerned at the dramatic change.

"Are you all right?" he asked sympathetically.

The old man nodded and straightened up.

"I'm sorry, forgive me. Jake was my grandson. The joy of my life. It happened so suddenly. He fell from a tree."

Chris found it hard to know what to say; he did not want to seem insensitive. Mr Watson pulled himself together and gave a great sigh.

"Poor little Rosie was heartbroken. Bless her – I'll never forget that she wanted her tin pencil box to go in the coffin with Jake. Such a touching gesture, but in all the upset it was forgotten. She carried it around with her for days after the funeral. I don't know what happened to the box after that."

Desperate to avoid an awkward silence and hoping talking would help, Chris ventured to ask if Jake's parent's were still here. He was told that they had moved to another position down south soon afterwards to get over their grief.

"But you stayed."

The gardener nodded, offering a tentative smile, as if to say, where else would he want to be? The conversation had come to its natural conclusion, and a dazed Chris took his leave.

He sat in the car for ages, still taking it all in. There was so much information whirling in his brain. He felt stunned. He had learned more about Rosie from that old man in a few minutes than in all the many years he had known her. None of this had even come out during Aunt Mary's recent conversation to Bridget. Was Bridget in for a shock! Rosie being artistic, like her!

He might not have been interested in Bridget's original information about Rosie, but now he was more than curious. No one who was that keen on drawing would simply turn her back on it like that. Bridget's obsession proved that. So why? Yet if something so unpleasant had happened here, why would Rosie have been determined to keep coming back? That did not make sense. There had to be more to this.

He needed to talk it over with Bridget before he went to see Aunt Mary. As soon as his sister answered her mobile, he told her about Rosie's drawings and the loss of her childhood friend. Bridget listened in awe, finding the whole thing incredible. There was one thing they agreed on; the initial alarm their aunt had shown when she learnt about the trip to Aston Hall was only half the story.

And what about Rosie, this child who had never talked about this part of her life? Did anyone really know her deepest feelings about the past? Did she keep going back because she wanted to share the same memories with someone special, if she could find him – the gardener, George Watson?

Chris stopped off in the village to buy flowers for his aunt and to give himself a little more time to think. His aunt had been was looking forward to his visit; she had said she would enjoy his company since the house was suddenly empty and quiet without either of his cousins. He did not mind spending time with her, but this afternoon's discovery had him a little concerned about how he was going to handle this visit.

Chris arrived at his aunt's home smiling reassuringly, but still unsure if he should say anything. Yet his curiosity had to be satisfied.

"Did Rosie like to draw? Most children do," he began casually as he hung up his coat. "The grounds of Aston Hall are a picture. I sent a lot of photos to Paula. I can't believe Rosie wasn't inspired by her surroundings."

This obviously surprised his aunt, as she stopped what she was doing.

"Yes, she did draw before, but she gave it up when she came here."

It seemed that was all he was going to get.

"Were the sketches any good?"

"Oh, yes. I tried to encourage her to continue, without any success. Eventually I had no choice but to put her favourite battered sketch pad and colouring pencils away in the attic with the other toys she refused to acknowledge."

"And Callum, did he ever see them?"

"I doubt it."

Ok. That was one question solved. Now for the next.

"Tell me, who was Jake?"

His aunt stared at him, clearly shocked by his words. Then she sat down. Chris made her a cup of sweet tea, handed it to her and gave her hand a comforting squeeze.

"I called into Aston Hall on a whim on the way here," he explained. "I bumped into an old gardener who had known Rosie and Jake and seen them play on the estate."

"I never expected..."

"Would you be able to tell me what happened?" Chris asked gently. Since the old man had made no secret of it, there was no need for her to, he reasoned.

She shuddered and shook her head, then spoke slowly. "Jake was Rosie's constant friend on the estate, but he died after falling from a tree. He was found one morning by one of the keepers. It was shocking, awful. Everyone was so upset. Rosie missed him so terribly. She never spoke about him after his death. Instead, she wandered about the place as if she was waiting for him to come back. Which was why her parents considered moving away, to help to her recover. Then there was that tragic road accident."

She paused. Chris patiently waited; he did not want to pressure her in any way, as it might stop her from telling him more.

"When she cried herself to sleep in my arms, I knew it was for Jake as well as her parents. Rosie never spoke his name and I learnt not to invade her silences. I left it for her to mention the past if she wanted, but she never did."

Chris could hear the deep emotion in her voice. There was no doubt she had done her best for Rosie and loved her.

"I didn't want her to be reminded of those nasty or painful memories all over again, which was why I was so surprised that she had enjoyed the visit to Aston Hall. It obviously didn't do any harm, because she has been back several times."

A little time passed before she spoke again.

"Why do *you* think did she wanted to go back so often? Did she miss it that much? Were we wrong not to take her there?"

Chris was reluctant to mention his own theory, which had been building the longer he thought about it. The grounds were enticing enough, he could understand the draw to reconnect with her childhood, but perhaps Rosie was looking for someone she thought would still be there with the same memories – someone who understood her time there with Jake? Maybe she was trying to find Jake's grandfather.

"I don't know. She has already come to terms with the past. She seems to be managing fine," Chris offered, keeping his other thoughts to himself.

With his aunt almost herself again, it had allowed Chris to attempt a question.

"How much does Callum know about Jake?"

"Nothing," she sighed. "There was never any need."

Common sense warned him to leave this alone. He did not need to dig anymore.

It took ages to sleep that night. His over-active brain was over-analysing everything. Chris could see a mass of complications ahead. It was bound to come out eventually with a whole heap of trouble all round. He had no idea how this was going to work out.

Chris's head was still churning in the morning, and he had a headache. His aunt looked as tired as he felt. They were both subdued and during the late breakfast they avoided returning to the topic of the previous day. Yet the expressions on their faces were enough to reveal what they were both thinking about.

He finished his final slice of toast, drained his cup and prepared to gently make his farewell. He was sorry he had turned this causal overnight stay into stirring up an unpleasant time, sorry he was leaving his aunt to come to terms with it all again. Let alone having to possibly deal with Callum at some point. He did not envy her that.

"I'm sorry," he said.

"Do you think this man you found is important to her?" she had to ask.

Chris shrugged. "We can only wait and see."

Chris arrived at the office the next morning ready for the usual hectic hustle and bustle of the *Despatch*'s newsroom.

He would also have to check some research for this special feature about the Marshall Theatre.

Cherry was looking over his shoulder and leaning on the chair, enquiring what he was covering. He showed her the draft profile of the last owner of the theatre and all the old press cuttings, explaining that he had arranged to meet Alfred James, the present caretaker-manager, for more memorabilia before the site was sold.

"It's a shame such buildings have to be lost," he said. "It will probably be demolished and redeveloped into some dreadful modern office block or flats."

Cherry nudged him. "I think you're getting too philosophical in your declining years," she said with a mischievous grin. At which he pushed her off the chair.

"But you are the oldest in the office," she pointed out.

If he could have found something suitable near at hand, he would have thrown it at her. Instead, he merely snarled theatrically, at which she stuck out her tongue at him and left.

Chris headed to the theatre that afternoon to interview the last remaining staff and Mr James, the caretaker-manager. He found himself planning the article as he walked from the nearest tube station. Nathan Ash, their photographer, had already been and had taken some shots inside.

The façade was certainly run down and it looked gloomy enough to make the odd passer-by stop to stare. As he approached the building, one solitary figure, a woman who was standing outside, seemed particularly mesmerised by its dilapidated appearance. As if trying to capture every detail, she was tilting her head up and down, moving slowly to take in all the details.

As Chris got closer he caught a proper look at her and stopped in astonishment. What! Surely not. Why on earth would the feisty Francesca be here in England of all places, studying this theatre? But there she was, only a few feet away from him. She was dressed less casually than before, with her tousled hair pulled back into a stylish thick plait that hung down her back. It made her look quite different. This was crazy! Dare he speak to her?

"Er, hello," he began.

She barely gave him a glance, still preoccupied with the theatre.

So he tried again. "I'm writing an article on the theatre for my newspaper, the *Despatch*. I have an interview with the manager."

"It deserves to be remembered kindly," she sighed, still perusing the façade.

"Not many theatres survive these days." He was hoping to extend this conversation.

"It used to be a fine venue," she said. He was surprised by the soft, gentle way she spoke.

"It's such a shame it could not be saved," he said.

"It's a lost cause. It's time to let it go. It's had its day. Everyone has wasted too much time and energy on trying to save it."

Her words indicated that she obviously knew more about this theatre than he had expected. But how? Had she lived in England before? It was hard to imagine her, of all people, having any connection to this theatre.

Francesca stepped into the foyer, still immersed in her own thoughts. He followed her slowly inside, where she disappeared through one of the many doors into the auditorium.

Mr James was waiting to greet him by the ticket booth, and proudly swept him away on a tour of the theatre. Chris had a job to do and spent quite a time taking notes from him and various other personnel he was introduced to. He did not want leave any interesting anecdote out of his article. This would be the last chance to record the theatre's history. He tried to listen attentively to everything Mr James told him, but he could not help being distracted now and again as Francesca wandered unhindered around the interior of the theatre. From the stage he saw her slowly stroll about the auditorium, running her fingers along the tops of the seats, touching various surfaces and looking around before making her way up the stairs to the balcony, where she sat for a while looking down at the stage.

Later, when he reached the top floor with his escort, who was still talking at a rapid rate, Chris saw her again. This time she lingered by the coloured glass window panels before entering a big office to stand facing a sturdy desk. No one seemed to be bothered by her presence here. She was obviously one of the theatre's insiders. Chris could not ignore it, he had to ask.

"The young lady who was just here, seems to know the theatre quite well."

"Yes. That's Francesca Lawson. Her father used to bring her here all the time."

Chris finished the interview, shoved his notebook into his pocket and strolled briskly out into the daylight. As he hurried back to the office he could not help wondering if Francesca was still inside. He idly wondered how long she had lived in England before moving to the sun. He was secretly convinced that this had been a personal pilgrimage for her. No doubt her father had worked here in some capacity, which was why she had some fondness for the place. But to travel all this way to England?

He returned with his notepad to the office, typed up what he had and settled down to check the internet archives for anything else he might have missed. He already had all the facts on the last owner, one Henry Marshall, who had invested heavily to keep it going.

He had been married to a former opera star, Jean Miller, that being her stage name. Chris punched her name into the search box. A few press reviews flipped onto the screen, a brief career resumé of her success in Europe and her many overseas tours. She had been quite famous. There was an old newspaper photo of her taken years ago, when she was in her prime.

There was also a photo of a villa she had bought in Sardinia as a private retreat. He enlarged the image. Chris stared at the picture; there was no mistaking it.

"Wow!" he exclaimed. He sat back from the computer screen, somewhat shocked by his discovery. It was the same beautiful white villa he had seen and taken photos of, behind the hotel. Jean Miller had lived there!

His eyes crinkled appreciatively. He was secretly pleased that someone else had continued to lavish the same loving care and attention on the house and garden that the original picture showed. It was reassuring in this day and age that it was still cherished.

He would have to tell Paula; she would be enthralled at the idea of the garden belonging to someone famous. He would send her copies of the two pictures he had just found, to go with those he had sent her previously.

Chris did not give much more thought to Francesca's presence at the theatre as he formulated his final layout for the glossy monthly magazine. He cut and pasted paragraphs to improve the basic draft, then flipped through the internet stuff he had saved to see what else he could use. He brought up the picture of Jean Miller and the villa again, and stared absently at it for a while. It looked such a magical place. He wondered how long she had lived there before returning permanently to England with Henry. Not that it was important.

He gazed sympathetically at the earlier pictures of them. The singer's face, the turn of the head as she faced the camera, the tilt of the chin and those dancing bright eyes. He felt he almost knew her. Her features reminded him of someone else. Why he was seeing something he had not seen before. He looked harder… Francesca! There was certainly a likeness.

He could not stop gazing at the screen. Francesca was just the daughter of a former employee of the Marshall Theatre, someone whose memories had brought her back for one last look at the building. Nothing more.

Cherry returned with a coffee to find Chris still staring at his screen, and dragged her chair up next to his.

"Penny for them," Cherry joked.

"I was thinking. The woman I met outside the theatre seemed really familiar with the building. I was wondering if she had some more interesting snippets I could use."

He knew he did not need to improve his copy. It was an excuse. He was puzzled by her sudden appearance there, despite having convinced himself previously that it was perfectly normal. The anomaly of the villa being so close to the hotel felt like more than mere coincidence. His curiosity had to be satisfied. He rolled his eyes to the ceiling and back.

"It's too late to add anything, we go to press tomorrow," said Cherry.

"I could do a follow up. It wouldn't hurt to talk to her. You never know," Chris declared firmly.

"Haven't you got enough to do? You don't usually waste your time on useless whims. Why chase after a perfect stranger who probably has nothing worth contributing?"

Francesca was not a stranger, but he could not tell Cherry that.

CHAPTER 5

A few days later, Matt phoned Bridget again. "I just wondered if I could see you again some time," he said.

"I thought you'd gone off the idea of us seeing each other any more," she pointed out. "You had better have a good reason for the way you've behaved."

"Sorry. I don't like being stared at. Sorry I am so awkward with these crutches," came his muttered reply.

"Is that all you have to say? What a pathetic excuse."

"Yes, I..."

But she did not allow him to continue. She went on to calmly inform him that she was busy this week, and at the weekend she would be looking after her nephews while their parents were away for an anniversary treat. He mumbled some vague words indicating he understood, and let her hang up. At least she had not told him to get lost, which was hopeful. Maybe.

"I don't know where I stand," Matt complained to Mike.

"No fledgling relationship ever runs smoothly," his brother reminded him.

Matt knew his over-defensive manner was getting in the way of the relationship. But he was trying.

Chris had just finished his weekend food shop at the supermarket when Mal dashed across the car park to join him. "Could you pop round later? I want to pick your brains."

Chris raised his eyebrows. This was a first.

"Wow. Do I get a consultancy fee?" he joked.

From Mal's expression, Chris decided that maybe not.

"What's up?" Chris asked on arrival at his home.

"You know people in your job, don't you?"

"What type of people?"

"Experts who deal with antique toys?"

"No, but I can ask around. Why, what's the problem?"

Mal told him about a neighbour, Maisie Cooper, who had inherited a vacant shop from a distant relation. She had been quite excited about it, but Mr Garrett, the solicitor who handed over the keys and the legal documents, seemed too keen to suggest that she sold it quickly. She did not like his insistence that being an old building, it would want a lot of repair and that a quick sale would save her the expense of the building work. It seemed too obvious that he had someone lined up to buy it cheap and make a profit.

"I went with her to inspect the shop immediately. The place was derelict, doors and floors creaked, and the shelves were all empty, with years of dust covering everything. But it did have charm, with old-fashioned brass handles, and bottle-glass windows. It could be a wonderful investment if it was restored properly. Honestly it could."

Mal was clearly excited. His face was glowing, and his eyes danced around to emphasise his words.

"Then there's the workshop at the rear. It's sound and fully equipped with all sorts of tools. They just need a clean and an oil. But – and this is the important part – there are boxes and boxes of unsold toys stored in the back. Not just any old toys, there are prime examples of working models, mechanical wind-up animals, character string puppets. You have to see them. Maisie doesn't seem to realise their potential worth and I was reluctant to build up her hopes."

Chris was listening intently, wondering if Mal was right.

"It is obvious this Garrett chap must have been in there at some point and had a good look around. Otherwise, why would he be so keen to get Maisie to sell? I tell you that stock needs to be valued by experts as soon as possible."

It certainly sounded that way to Chris.

"At least she has had the sense to get the locks changed straight away," Mal continued.

"But you're still worried."

Mal nodded. "How can we stop Garrett getting the toys or influencing the sale? Is there anything we can do?"

One of Chris's pet hates was people being cheated or scammed by unscrupulous individuals. This sounded urgent; he had to think of something.

"I think the answer is a pleasant social visit to Mr Garrett, as soon as possible."

"But what good can that do? He's hardly likely to admit he's on the make."

"The meeting will concern the paper's next feature. We don't let him think we suspect anything. We don't challenge him at all."

Mal looked stumped, but Chris was grinning as a subtle plan began to formulate. Chris was not adverse to a bit of skulduggery to achieve what he had in mind.

They met outside the solicitor's office on the Monday morning, after Chris had persuaded Alan to cover for him for a couple of hours. Then Chris gave Mal his instructions.

"I want you to follow my lead, back me up. And go along with whatever I say."

Mal nodded. He was going to enjoy this. He had no idea how it was going to go down, but he trusted Chris.

Shown into Mr Garrett's office, Chris introduced himself and showed his press ID, indicating that Mal was the paper's photographer.

"Good morning, Mr Garrett. As I explained on the phone to you earlier. I have a deadline to meet, which is why

I had to speak to you today."

"Anything I can do to help," replied the man behind the desk, who was plump with a chubby face and greying hair.

"I write features for a magazine. I heard about the Old Toy Shop in the High Street, which has stood unused for years. I think it would of great interest. A well-deserved splash of publicity would highlight its potential. It's about time it was brought to the attention of the public."

"The... Old Toy Shop?" stuttered Mr Garrett, clearly startled.

Chris was experienced at reading people, every flick of the eyes, the turn away glance, the nervous twitch. The reluctant sigh. Chris had the man summed up in seconds.

"Yes, yes. The place is a gem. There are so many antique toys in there. I have contacted an expert in that field, and he is doing a detailed inventory for valuation today and tomorrow. My associate here has taken photos of everything. We don't want anything to go missing in the process."

"You have been inside? You have taken *photos?*"

Mr Garrett's facial movements and body language were exactly as Chris had expected. He looked unsettled and on edge.

Mal nodded. "Oh yes, as soon as she had the keys Mrs Cooper showed us around. She had no idea of the actual contents under all the dirt and cobwebs. What a find."

"She certainly can't sell the shop until these toys are catalogued and valued," Chris added brightly. "Even then she will need professional guidance. But for the moment she has been savvy enough to have the locks changed and a security system installed."

"Very, er, wise," the lawyer agreed. His face was pale and his forehead was beaded with sweat.

"We have some highly recommended legal advisors on hand, if she wants their assistance."

"So why did you need to speak to me?" The solicitor was looking baffled.

"Ah yes. What I really need is some history about the previous owner of the building. I have some basic archive data on the actual bricks and mortar and old black and white photos, but little about the man himself. Mrs Cooper had no personal reminisces of the relative who had left her the shop, and most of his old friends seemed to have passed away. We have spoken to the locals, but we haven't had much luck. Since he was your client, I hoped you might have some information."

Mr Garrett appeared to give this a little thought, although Chris could tell that all he wanted was to get rid of them. He told Chris that he had not seen the client much in recent years. All he knew was that the old man had loved woodwork in his younger days, making things in the workshop at the rear and repairing toys for the children. But he had never made enough money to keep it as a going concern, which was why he had closed the shop. It had remained empty and unused, while he had become a recluse living above it.

"Well, thank you for your time," said Chris. "I really want

to get this out in the next issue, unless someone else submits a better story first, of course."

Mal followed Chris outside and down the steps. He could not wait to tackle him once they were out of sight of Mr Garrett's office.

"Do you think that worked?" he asked.

"By the look on his face, we've scared him witless. I don't think he would be stupid enough to try anything now."

They shook hands on their successful ruse.

"So, I'd better set about getting all these proposals into motion." Chris grinned.

"I thought it was just a bluff."

"Maybe it was, but we can't let her down now."

"Thanks Chris."

Chris felt gratified that they had outsmarted the devious Mr Garrett, and there was no reason why the story could not indeed go in the next issue. The Old Toy Shop would make a fresh change to their usual type of feature. He could not wait to begin the tasks he had just outlined, the first being to get Nathan to photograph everything. In fact, he was keen to see the photos of the toys for himself. No doubt Bridget would also appreciate them.

Of course, the whole matter reminded him of Rosie and her toys in the attic, never used, never touched, which in turn made him wonder how things were in his aunt's house, now Rosie and Callum would be back from their trips.

He soon found out. Instead of his aunt speaking when he

phoned, a sullen Callum answered. "Rosie's back at Aston Hall," he said. With only a week left before Callum went back to university, his growing frustration echoed down the phone. He had to talk to someone. Rosie had come in one day, absolutely delighted, announcing that she had found someone she knew at Aston Estate. Since Rosie had found the old gardener, there were no more confidences or idle friendly banter between them. It was not the same; he was feeling left out, and he sulked. They seemed to be drifting apart when they had once had been so close.

Chris was immediately aware that Callum had not said 'Jake's grandfather'; he had merely referred to him as 'the old gardener'. Did this mean he had still not been told about Jake? Chris would have to be careful what he said. He listened patiently and let his cousin rant on until he ran out of things to say before trying to ease the situation.

"It's hardly surprising they spent so much time together, when they have years to catch up on between them. Please don't spoil it for her."

There was no need to talk to Aunt Mary now; Callum had told him all he wanted to know, so he was surprised when Aunt Mary immediately phoning him afterwards. She admitted she was worried about Rosie's new fascination with George Watson, and Callum's sulking because she no longer wanted his company. She feared that they would not patch up their differences before they went back to their studies.

"I'm sure they will come to their senses," said Chris, in a poor attempt to ease her mind.

There was a long pause at Aunt Mary's end of the phone. Chris did not know what else to say to cheer her up. He pulled a face.

In a quieter moment, Bridget and Chris managed to discussed the problem afresh. There was no doubt Rosie would see Mr Watson again as often as she could, and eventually Callum would find out the rest. It was inevitable.

"We can't make Rosie tell him about Jake," Chris pointed out.

"Some things are just too precious to share," said Bridget.

"Very philosophical," Chris commented. Even he only learnt things about Matt on Bridget's terms.

For once Chris was enjoying a peaceful weekend. He lay in, had a late cooked breakfast, did a few chores and settled down to indulge himself by reading a few more chapters of a book. Later, in a mellow reflective mood, he returned to some of his own fond memories. He found himself looking through the old photo albums and playing a song which reminded him of Ellen, the Garth Brooks song *What's She Doing Now*. He often wondered where she was and what she was up to. No doubt still wandering the globe, by the odd postcard she sent him; they decorated the back of the kitchen door, next to the calendar. He smiled to himself, pleased to think he still had a wife somewhere. He wished she would come home, although he had no way of telling her that. If he closed his eyes, he could still feel her touch and smell her shampoo. He would have to be content with that.

Matt phoned Bridget again. It had been ages, or it seemed like it. She refused again, blaming work commitments. She was busily planning a presentation for their next project, and she and her partner were rushing about arranging details and dealing with suppliers. This was important. He would have to wait.

At least she had been willing to chat to him. That was a positive sign, wasn't it? So, he asked when he could see her again, wondering if he was pushing his luck. To be told that maybe he could try next week. That glimmer of hope bounded back.

"But your ideas for our outings will have to be improved on."

Matt didn't mind what they did together. Well – he was not about to run a marathon. But Bridget was setting the rules and he would have to shape up to be what she expected if he wanted to rebuild their friendship.

Then in the next breath, because she could hardly help herself, because she was so excited, she was telling him all about the Fairfax site and what was involved. She was commuting to Fairfax Hall and back, every day. She did have to work for a living, she reminded him. Which could have been taken as a less than subtle hint that he should be doing something about his own future.

Matt knew he had to find a way forward. He was still at

the farm, getting under his parents' feet. He had wandered around his childhood home and down to the village, trying to find the answer. He needed to find a house and a job, but where, and what could he do? It was not as if he was ignoring the problem. He honestly did not know what career path he wanted to follow. Whatever it was, it would mean retraining. Starting again was a daunting prospect. What interested him? Nothing much at the moment. Nothing grabbed his attention; he could not settle for a mundane job, that was clear. He had discussed this with his father without success. Realistically he could not make any decision until his leg was better. He had been told the bones could take months to regain their normal strength. It seemed forever. He had already set himself the goal of driving their old bone-rattling tractor round the farm. When he had achieved that, he would buy himself a nippy second-hand car to be more independent. Then he would be fit enough to challenge anything.

Chris contacted Bridget to find out if he was still taking her out for a meal on her birthday, or if she was doing something special with Matt that day. She giggled and admitted that she had not even told Matt when her birthday was. Besides, at the moment she did not want to break the routine of having her brother make a fuss of her. She enjoyed it so much.

Since Chris was free to spoil her, he asked her if she would prefer an afternoon tea somewhere posh or an evening meal. The evening meal won. He could not resist teasing her by saying that with Matt being out of work, he doubted if he could afford to treat her anyway. She huffed and told him not to be so mean. Yet the remark was echoed during her next visit to Paula and Ray.

Bridget resisted all the obvious roundabout questions concerning Matt from both Paula and Ray, together with the usual gentle teasing from her brother-in-law concerning her choice of boyfriend. A moment ago he had joked that it was about time this Matt wined and dined her properly, despite his injury.

"Can't he afford to take you somewhere nice?" Ray added, collecting his newspaper from the hall.

"Ray!"

"Ouch!" he grunted as his wife hit him.

Bridget strolled idly into the kitchen to check the kettle, considering Ray's idea. When she next spoke to Matt, she would suggest that they could go out to dinner somewhere quiet and see what he said. It did not matter where, it did not need to be posh or expensive, just somewhere nice, would make a change.

"Since you're giving Matt a second chance, why don't you invite him come to watch the 5k fun run in Maidstone with us on Saturday?" Paula asked.

"Unless the idea of meeting our terrible children might put him off?" Ray added.

The idea sounded fine, except the crowds might be a problem for him to cope with on his crutches, plus he had certainly never talked about any sport in the time she had known him.

"I don't think he is particularly interested in sport."

"What man doesn't follow some sport or other?" Ray gasped, unable to comprehend such a concept. "Well, except for your brother," he conceded as an afterthought.

Bridget shrugged, promising she would put the proposition to Matt when she got home.

A less than hopeful Bridget phoned him later. Matt gave an awkward sigh. Him, anywhere near a sporting venue? Not likely. How was he going to get out of this? He was not really a sports follower, he waffled weakly, adding that he did not even watching sport on the television. He stopped as he heard her draw breath at the other end.

"Fine. So how about meeting us later after the event is over instead?"

Matt had to scupper that idea as well. The crowds were bound to linger for ages, there would be hordes of excited parents and children underfoot. He wasn't sure he could manage. It would be different when he was fit again, he promised.

"It had better be," she told him. "A little give and take would not go amiss."

She put the phone down, having forgotten all about her

intention to mention going out to dinner. She was not in the mood now, anyway.

Meanwhile, Chris had stopped at the Marriott Hotel on his way back from an assignment and had called in to make a dinner booking. His sister's birthday treat was an occasion he did not dare to mess up. He checked the menu and requested a table by the window, which he knew would be a favourite spot. Everything was perfectly arranged.

As he wandered out of the restaurant, he had a surprise; Francesca. He had not expected to see her again and had assumed she had gone back to Sardinia. He had not thought there was anything to keep her here after visiting the theatre, but there she was, looking very smart and businesslike and looking completely at home on the phone behind the front desk. Chris half-smiled as he made his way out into the street. He was pleased to think that she had established a career here in London, away from the temptation of Italy.

It was not long before Chris saw his sister again, for she called in on her way home. She threw her bag on the settee, looking miffed. After talking to Paula, she would often find the time to complain to Chris as well, goodness knows why. She was scowling.

"The charity fun run in Mote Park is scheduled for Saturday," she said. "I had hoped to persuade Matt to meet Paula and Ray then, since he is convalescing at his parents' farm near Charing and they don't live too far from

Maidstone, it seemed a good idea to fix something up."

"Oh fine, you don't want him to meet me then?" Chris was quick to put in.

"No."

"Well thanks. You do know how to make a brother feel unwanted." He grunted in mock indignation.

"He doesn't like the press. Anyway, that's not the point. His excuse is that he says he's going through a bad patch."

"And you don't believe him."

"No. I don't," she growled. "Bloody Matt."

Chris was startled. He had never heard his sister swear before.

"Maybe he is going a through a bad patch, Bridget. It might be difficult for him. Then there is the added deterrent of our boisterous nephews to contend with."

Personally Chris felt she had not thought this through. Some poor guy on crutches, struggling to manage in that crowd – making him do that did not seem very fair. Why had she expected him to agree?

"Don't you dare make excuses for him. It wouldn't be that difficult. I only wanted to introduce him to them after the fun run or call in at their place for a few minutes".

Where did this sudden 'meeting the family' idea come from, he wondered. That stage usually came later, once they were a definite item. Which they did not look like at present.

It was nothing like that, she insisted. It was only because she had met his brother Mike early on and kept seeing him frequently, mainly because he was Matt's chauffeur most of the time. She felt she should reciprocate by having Matt meet part of her family.

Chris shrugged. It seemed logical. He did not really mind being sidelined. In fact it might be safer not to get involved.

"And is Mike as evasive as Matt?" he asked.

"Well, clever clogs, it just so happens that he isn't. He's an officer in the Metropolitan Police and he's always very friendly. He's doing his best to get Matt out of this rut he's in."

Good luck with that then, Chris thought to himself. Matt's brother must have the patience of a saint. Fitting in all his spare time into ferrying his brother around must be difficult, in his job. On top of which Chris had gathered that he accompanied Matt to the private physiotherapist, to provide moral support. Brotherly devotion did not cover it. Maybe there *was* something special about Matt, something that no one else knew.

Bridget went on to add, more than a little sarcastically, that due to Matt's aversion to crowds, she would think twice about inviting him anywhere in future. Chris knew she didn't mean it; he knew his sister, knew she was not going to give up on him yet. But he could not help wondering about her tentative relationship. Where was it going wrong? His own romance had been one long easy blend of affection, trust and understanding. Theirs was – who could describe it?

After the latest rift concerning his refusal to join her at the Maidstone Fun Run, Matt felt he had to attempt to ease the problem. A little of the truth might swing it. It was worth a try. He explained that apart from being overwhelmed by the mass of people, the last thing he wanted was to watch athletes, because, silly as it was, it would make him feel uncomfortable and embarrassed at his own inadequacies. There, he had at last been openly honest with her.

Bridget went very quiet. She could hear the truth in his voice and knew it must have been hard for him to say. She let out a rueful sigh, voicing her own regret at being so hard on him. She admitted she must learn to be more tolerant and less judgmental, when she was far from perfect herself. While the family were used to her being totally engrossed in her artistic activities, switching off from any outside influences, no doubt Matt would find it hard to understand.

Not long after, Matt was feeling over the moon. At last the plaster cast had been removed, an enormous step forward. He did not mind that it had been replaced by a clip-on lightweight plastic calliper to be worn during the day as a precaution. That and a simple walking stick made him feel more human again. He was so relieved.

Matt practised for hours up and down the quiet towpath, much to his father's annoyance, in an effort to correct the limp he seemed to have been be left with. The specialist physiotherapist had strictly warned him about the danger of over exercising. Although the bones were fine, the sessions to strengthen the muscles to support the damaged bones were still critical and should be done gradually. But Matt, being Matt, was determined to manage without his advice.

Matt soon learnt he had ignored his father's concern at his peril. Thanks to his intervention he found himself summoned back to the hospital. There in the consultant surgeon's office, he received a severe rollicking and a dire warning. Over-exercise would weaken the muscles, not strengthen them. He could cause irreparable damage. He had a choice: he either slowed down or he would be taken back into hospital, immediately.

Matt looked from the consultant to his father, who did not seem surprised at this ultimatum. He folded his arms and gave his son a look that said, 'I told you'. Matt conceded. Going back into hospital was out of the question. He had not forgotten those first weeks when he had been immobilised, waiting for the swelling to go down. Frustrated, he gave a nod of acceptance and promised to follow the strict guidelines he was issued. He was impatient to be properly fit again. He was eager to show off his improvement to Bridget. She had become important; she was more than nice to be with, she was funny, practical and down to earth, and she could quote Shakespeare. Most of all he adored the way her nose crinkled whenever she was teasing him.

Then he did something quite unexpected, as if he knew what she had had in mind. He phoned her to say he had booked a meal for them both at a charming little restaurant called Le Bistro. A taxi would take them there and collect them afterwards. He hoped he had thought of everything.

He would devote more time to taking her out properly, he promised.

He could even wear one of those expensive suits from the London flat – or was that too much? Perhaps. Instead he invested in smart new trousers and a jacket, hoping Bridget would appreciate the new him. He could not wait to collect her for their date, or to see the surprise on her face.

Seeing Francesca at the hotel made Chris think more about her. He had already been aware of her likeness to the late Jean Miller but having convinced himself she was the daughter of a former employee of the Marshall Theatre, he needed to see that photo of Jean again, to test if his imagination was playing tricks.

He was in the office early the next morning, attempting to do his research in private. It did not work. Cherry arrived minutes later and sat watching him as he brought up his documents. She had worked with him too long not to recognise that frown of intense curiosity.

"What are you really up to, Batman?"

"The girl I spoke to outside the theatre. I think she could be Jean Miller's daughter."

"After one short meeting? That is some jump to make. And even if she was, what does it matter?"

He could not answer that immediately; he was still thinking. Were they related? Was she in fact the late Jean and Henry Marshall's daughter? How could that be? There was no mention in his research of them having a daughter.

Their surnames were different, but what was in a name? Yet he had seen her on the road to the white villa, Jean Miller's home in Sardinia and at the theatre. It would explain her reason for being at the theatre and her attachment to the place. Was the link too much of a coincidence?

"There could be more to this story."

Cherry considered everything for a moment before giving her opinion.

"Christopher, don't be so stupid. Forget it. Let it go. There's no point in interviewing her for some personal gossip, because that's all it would be. Meaningless gossip."

But she could see that he was still considering the idea. This was getting troublesome. She had promised, at Francesca's request, to keep their friendship a secret, in order to protect Francesca's private life. It was time to stop him making what she saw as an obvious mistake. She was on her high horse now, and really annoyed with him.

"And have you considered that that might be the last thing she would want? Even if her parents were Jean Miller and Henry Marshall, she may want to keep their lives private. Why should she want to have her personal memories and her name plastered across the press? And another thing. Why would she want to talk to you? Besides, how would you get in touch with her?"

Chris did not reply, because he had that covered. Unknown to anyone he had two leads, the theatre manager and the Marriott Hotel, where she was presently working.

Cherry took his silence as a sign that she had won her

point. "You're an idiot," she huffed. Had she said enough? She hoped so.

Idiot or not, Chris contacted Mr James, the caretaker-manager of the Marshall Theatre, the next day. On the pretext of possibly doing a further follow-up article, he asked the important question first. Was Miss Lawson related to Jean Miller and Henry Marshall?

The affirmative answer had him asking several other important questions. What did Mr James think about getting an interview with her about the theatre? He saw no reason in why not. Good. Could he put him in touch with her? Mr James was most obliging and readily passed on Francesca's phone number. Chris could not believe his luck.

He waited a few minutes to collect his thoughts. Should he do this? What the heck, it wouldn't hurt anyone. He would give it a try; she could only say no.

When he dialled the number, he was a little thrown to find that it went straight to Francesca's personal secretary. He now found himself dealing with a formal business organisation. This was not what he had expected.

He enquired if he could be put through to Francesca – Miss Lawson, he corrected himself – to find himself immediately rebuffed. She was unavailable at the moment. Miss Lawson had an important meeting which could not be interrupted. Was there anyone else in the management team at the Marriott Hotel that he wished to speak to instead, the secretary asked.

"Er, no thank you. It's nothing to do with hotel business. I merely wished to have a brief chat with Miss Lawson about the Marshall Theatre."

He heard the woman grunt, clearly put out at being bothered with something so insignificant. She was obviously used to dealing with more important matters. She mumbled begrudgingly that she would enquire for him when Miss Lawson returned later, although she was very doubtful that Miss Lawson would agree. It depended if she had a free slot in her schedule, in which case she would phone him back to make an appointment.

Chris accepted her offer, as there was no point in pleading his case or explaining that he simply hoped for some additional insight concerning the article he had already published. He would be wasting his breath. Should he forget it? Francesca might not agree to see him once she heard his name, anyway.

Chris was still stunned by this totally different perception of Francesca. Her position as a prominent executive for a prestigious hotel chain could not have been achieved overnight. She must have been established in her career for some time. So much for the feisty in-your-face antagonist, the flirtation with a married man and the sentimental feeling for the theatre. All those perceptions were only part of her character. It just goes to show, you can never tell about people, he concluded.

Bridget beamed with delight at Matt's improved appearance.

She could almost have hugged him. He looked more positive, brighter and a good deal better than before. He also looked more charming and handsome, despite the short beard he had refused to shave off. Not that she had given up on that yet.

"I hated the slow progress I was making. I hated being me, a lot of the time," said Matt, feeling confident enough to open up a little more to her.

Bridget was impressed that he was making an effort to get out into the wide world. Their evening at Le Bistro turned out to be delightful, thanks to Matt's relaxed mood and close attention to her. The faultless, discreet service of the staff and the warm ambience of the setting made her feel special. The restaurant was intimate setting and quiet, well suited to the type of clientele who dined here.

She could not wait to tell Chris and Paula about her evening out and how Matt had done something quite unexpected and lovely. It had been such a wonderful time.

Once she had finished her bubbling account, Chris went to look it up, as he had never heard of the place. From the photos on the website it looked expensive and well out of his league, or his pocket. He could not help wondering if Matt had raided his savings to afford it.

When Chris mentioned the name of the restaurant to Jonathan, the acknowledged food and drink expert at work, he raised his eyebrows in surprise. He was impressed that this secret gem of the culinary world had been visited by his sister and her companion so casually. It was a very exclusive place, he told Chris. And when Chris mentioned that it had been almost empty, probably because it was a midweek booking, Jonathan almost laughed. Chris shrugged; maybe it was a coincidence that the bookings were low that particular night. Jonathan shook his head. That would be a first, he said. Its outstanding reputation made it most unlikely, and he went off to find out more about this strange occurrence. He returned less than half an hour later, looking pleased with himself, to give Chris the lowdown. It seemed some client, whom they would not identify, had requested that the numbers were limited that night and had paid very highly for the privilege. Indeed, his sister and her friend had been lucky to get in.

Chris was pleased to think they had been that fortunate. So it seemed that after a rocky start, Bridget's relationship with Matt seemed to be going in the right direction. Matt was beginning to prove his worth at last.

CHAPTER 6

Chris hoped the interview with Francesca would not be as difficult as Cherry had predicted. What would be the best approach? He had it all planned; he was going to be completely professional. He certainly wasn't going to mention Sardinia. He would keep to the point. His magazine article had already paid homage to the dedication of those who had made the Marshall Theatre a success, especially her dearly loved parents. He would mention the well-known stars whose careers had started here and include their reminiscences, then finish by mentioning the regrettable state of British theatre in general. He would ask her if she could add anything else, which he would be pleased to include in any future piece. He would tell her always appreciated any extra input that was offered.

When the secretary phoned back to let him know he could have an appointment for Friday, it seemed like ages away. He asked if it could be brought forward, but he was told it had been confirmed for that day, unless he wanted to cancel? God, no!

Until then he would have to hone his technique, hoping his professional attitude and civil manner would placate any residual hostility. He would tell her this was purely business and he just wanted to find out a few more facts about the theatre. Why was he really doing this? He already knew who her parents were. What else did he need to know? Nothing really. It was a personal whim, one he should not have given in to, but that was him all over.

He wanted the chance to see her in her new environment, to see how different she was. He could not help being impressed as he was escorted up in the private lift to a very imposing outer office. Here he waited to be ushered into an even smarter grand office, which appeared to be more like an international hotel lounge. It had leather armchairs, settees and glass-topped coffee tables, with bookshelves and ornaments taking up one wall, while her desk faced out of a floor-to-ceiling window with a view over London. He did not have much time to appreciate his surroundings as she indicated a comfortable chair for him to sit in.

"I read your article in the magazine," Francesca began, her tone relaxed.

"I hope Henry Marshall would have approved."

"I'm sure he would have."

Chris was intrigued. The tone of her voice and the way she had spoken indicated personal affection for the man. It confirmed all Chris had learnt from his prime source.

"I understand Mr Marshall was involved in the running of the theatre for many years."

"We tried to save it for so long, in his memory."

He was already running out of questions.

"Did you go to many of the performances?" he tried.

"Of course."

She happily recalled some of the numerous acts and stars she had seen, together with a couple of stories of things that had gone wrong behind the scenes, causing hilarious uproar in the theatre. Finally she stopped and smiled.

"I had a lovely childhood," she said.

How he wanted to ask about that. But how could he without being thrown out?

"Was any of that useful?"

"It's the little personal anecdotes that make articles more interesting for the reader. Thank you for your time."

They shook hands and she smiled amicably.

On his way to the door, he paused and turned back. "I hope you don't mind me saying. You are very like the archive picture of Jean Miller."

"So people often tell me." She sighed. He was much too level-headed to expect her to volunteer anything more.

Chris felt pleased with himself as he left. He had witnessed the warmth she felt about the theatre and the people who had worked there and her parents. Although she had not spoken about them directly, he could see it in her. There was a softer side to Francesca. There was more to her than he had encountered before. Since she obviously had a permanent base here in London, he could not help wondering if the white villa in Sardinia was her second home. Was she the one who tended it so lovingly? He hoped she was. His curiosity was bursting. Much good did it do him.

Paula's voice was full of mischief as she taunted Chris down the phone.

"I know something you don't."

"Come on then. This had better be good."

"Matt has a beard."

Was that it? It wasn't much. How did she know?

"Have you met him then?"

"No, silly. We're still waiting for that. The boys were on a school trip to London. They said they saw Bridget arm in arm with a good-looking bearded young man, who had a walking stick. I guess it was Matt."

"And you rang me just for that?"

"I thought you'd be interested."

"I would rather meet the guy in person."

"Likewise."

Although the information was nothing world shattering, it gave him something he could use to tease Bridget with the next time he saw her. Which he did with some enjoyment.

"You never said Matt had a beard."

Bridget frowned. "How did you know?"

"Two eagle-eyed nephews saw you from the coach on a school trip."

She laughed. "I've told him he would look more handsome without it."

Bridget had invited Rosie down over the half-term break for a weekend of shopping. While they were in London, she also intended to take her to the rebuilt Shakespeare's Globe Theatre. Chris immediately saw this as his opportunity for few private words with Rosie, by offering to act as a taxi to and from the station. Except he had hardly got a word in during the journey to Bridget's, because Rosie was too full of news about her college course. He decided he would call in at Bridget's place later.

So in the late afternoon, the girls arrived back from their shopping to find Chris already comfortably settled in Bridget's lounge, watching the television. While she busied herself in the kitchen, Rosie came to plonk herself down beside him.

"Jake's grandfather told me he spoke to you in the summer."

Chris nodded, drawing her closer. She snuggled up to him.

"He told me about Jake."

"I know," she said.

"If I had known about Jake on top of everything else, I would never have made you go to Aston Hall that day.

You should have said something. It must have been hard for you."

"Yes, I thought it would be too. I had missed Jake so much. Then there I was, in our home surroundings again and the sadness of his loss somehow changed into the fondest of memories. He was still there, his laughter and giggles echoed in the gardens where we played. It was as if his warm hand was in mine."

Chris gave her a hug. He was so glad she had told him.

"Then finding Jake's grandfather, was – wonderful."

She squeezed his hand and he reciprocated.

"You've been very diplomatic. I know you haven't told Callum about Jake."

"No, I haven't. But I suggest you tell him soon. He needs to know. Callum is already hurt that things are not the same between you. It could cause an irretrievable rift."

"I can't tell him about Jake. Jake belongs to me and his grandfather. No one else."

Chris could see that her deep affection for Jake was too private and as Bridget had said, too precious. It was held close within her, deep and strong. And she would fight to keep it there.

He took a deep breath. He had to try something to get things back on an even keel at Aunt Mary's home. He began his pitch by proposing that she could share something else. The drawings in the attic would be a start. Callum would appreciate that.

Her response was not enthusiastic, but she did not dismiss the idea.

"I suppose I have been selfish..."

"A little thoughtless, maybe."

Had he said enough? He couldn't tell.

When Bridget returned from the kitchen to discuss their purchases, Rosie gave her a smile and he sensed a long girlie chat was imminent. In which case it was definitely time to get out of here. He left the girls to enjoy themselves and promised to be on time tomorrow, to take Rosie and all her extra bags to the station.

Within days Callum was back on the phone, complaining that he had really lost his temper with Rosie when she told him that what she did these days was none of his business. Chris stared at the phone. So much for his little pep talk. That hadn't worked. How could life be so complicated?

"Ok Chris, you obviously must know something," said Callum. "Mother mentioned someone called Jake and then clammed up. Now I can't get any sense out of her and Rosie won't say. Who is this Jake?"

Chris took a deep breath and closed his eyes. Was it really up to him to explain? Fine, then he would. He would make it as simple as he could.

"I believe he was a childhood friend who died on the Aston Hall estate. They were very close."

His cousin was speechless for a moment before letting

out his fury about the fact that no one, not even his mother, had shared such earth-shattering news with him before.

"Callum, listen. The gardener, George Watson, is Jake's grandfather. They share Jake's memory. They need to talk it out before Rosie can move on. You will have to learn to be patient. I'm sure it's only a phase. Just give her a little more time."

"More time! A month? A year?" Callum grunted.

The lecture over, he conceded and the conversation fizzled out. Despite being a difficult conversation, at least most of it was out in the open now, Chris hoped.

Matt knew Bridget would be pleased at his becoming more sociable. He felt something comforting about his achievement, be it on his own terms. Although he still had not managed to drive the tractor, he would get there. He was getting used to being in public again, and no one noticed who he was these days, maybe because he still kept the beard and did not flaunt his name.

His latest suggestion for lunch at a riverside pub in Kent suited them both fine. His father could drop him off and since Bridget would be staying at her sister's overnight in Maidstone, she could easily drive there.

They took their drinks on to the terrace in the afternoon sun, where there was a sign announcing live music there at weekends. The same poster had been at the entrance when they arrived, and he could see she was considering the idea as she read the details. There was little doubt she would be up for coming back to see the bands.

"I used to see the Concerts in the Park years ago," she mused idly.

"Who did you see?" he asked.

"The Stones, Status Quo and then Queen – I suppose I'm out of touch now."

"Just a bit." He laughed. "I used to like the open-air concerts as well."

"And now?"

He made no effort to comment, giving the impression he was not particularly bothered.

"The way you looked at the poster, anyone would think you wanted to come here to hear that band," he said.

"I do. Don't you?"

He shrugged, deliberately keeping her guessing. But he could not keep it up when her face fell with disappointment. He leaned forward.

"Of course I do. Anything to be with you," he whispered in her ear.

She was delighted. He nudged her gently as they walked quietly back, his hand firmly holding hers.

Matt even found himself talking fondly of his own times at concerts, and enthusing over the buzz and excitement he had felt about just being in the crowd. He mentioned some lesser-known entertainers and seemed quite open about his visits to night clubs and wine bars, even admitting he had been a normal male out on the town. No saint, but no villain either, he concluded.

"You were a party animal then?" she teased.

"Sort of. But not for a long time now."

"We know what we are, but not what we may be." Bridget was quoting from Shakespeare. Did that sum him up, he wondered?

Their conversation had continued casually enough with Matt telling her about his decision to sell his flat and move out of London for good. He had not lived there for ages, in fact not ever since the accident. Everything was in boxes. He had appointments with the surveyor and several estate agents over the next couple of days. The money would come in useful for his fresh start.

"How long did you live in the city?" she asked.

"Only a couple of years."

"Won't you miss not being in the centre of things?"

"I've had my fill of all the bright lights and attractions of the capital."

"Men are sometimes masters of their fate," she quoted again.

But was he?

"You prefer to be a country boy again?"

He nodded nonchalantly. Bridget obviously liked that, and he did not mind that she had begun to draw little confidences out of him, although he still had to be cautious about exactly what he said. Their conversation was casual enough until she asked where the property was. He could hardly tell her it was an expensive pad in Richmond.

"Nowhere special," he said.

Chris could only shake his head at the pair of them as his sister complained. Again. He would have thought Matt would have learnt by now. And as for Bridget, now she had given it more thought she was contrite enough to admit that she should not have been so put out at his refusal to tell her. She had not considered that maybe he was ashamed to admit where it was. It could be some awful dive in a rundown area, in which case she had to forgive him.

A few hours later, Matt was still in a strange mood, unable to find anything to occupy his mind, the papers scattered on the floor, a book thrown on the table. He had not been prepared for the question about the flat, although he should have been since he had brought it up in the first place. There had been no quick lie to give her. Instead he had deliberately waffled, badly. What could he say this time? He picked up the phone.

"Hello Bridget. I – I wondered if..."

"Oh, I can't talk now."

She had stopped him in his tracks. Her business partner was picking her up from Paula's shortly, for an appointment in Lenham village, after which they would be heading back to London together.

She had not mentioned anything about his flat. Had she forgotten about it? Please?

"Now listen, you are coming to meet Paula and Ray next week," she said. "Unless you have something better to do with your time?"

There was a warning note in her tone. Did he have any choice?

So one week later, Matt prepared himself for the worst. He could not put it off any longer. He had to admit that he was more than slightly nervous; this would be his first real challenge, to face Bridget's family. But they were normal everyday people and unless they were avid news followers, he had every chance of getting away with it. At least the newshound was not included, and he had been promised the children would be kept out of the way. It was the children that worried him the most. Children were too perceptive, experience had taught him. He remembered the incident when he had had to abruptly turned away from those children, that day in the park. It was not his awkwardness with crutches in public which had been the problem, it was the potential scrutiny of the children as they stopped to stare at him. The stare which lingered too long.

Inside the house, Bridget's two nephews had raced downstairs, dashing to the front windows, pushing and nudging each other.

"Mum, Mum, come and look! Aunt Bridget's here with the new boyfriend!"

"Gosh!"

"Boys, come away from the front window. Let Bridget have some privacy," their mother ordered.

"But Mum!"

"Get back upstairs! This minute! And stay there," she instructed, in a tone that meant no argument.

Reluctantly they obeyed, with many a backward glance in case she changed her mind, but she stood at the foot of the stairs watching them and pointed to their rooms. Once they were out of the way, their parents went out to meet Bridget's new acquaintance.

"Hello Matt. I've been looking forward to meeting you," Paula purred.

Matt glanced nervously at her, unsure of any inference in her greeting.

"Don't take it personally. She likes to vet all her sister's boyfriends," Ray joked.

"Raaay!"

Ray pushed in. "Nice to meet you at last, Matt. How are you?"

There was no mistaking the sincerity of the handshake as Matt looked into Ray's beaming face, no sign that this was anything other than a normal greeting.

Introductions were made all round and polite general conversation continued over the usual cup of tea. Everything had been casual and friendly, and as they drove away later, Matt leaned back in his seat, half-smiling to himself. They had not recognised him; why would they? His face was not in the news any more.

This had been easier than he expected. It gave him a surge of confidence to think of his future again. A future with Bridget, if he was lucky. Yes, she mattered. He had not minded paying Le Bistro that exorbitant price to ensure their privacy for that exclusive meal with her. It had been worth every penny, and worth having to rest up the next day.

For Chris, life continued in the same routine. He had covered many different news stories over the months. News was news, whatever it was about. He was still feeling pleased with himself over the toy shop feature and for having a hand in outsmarting the shifty solicitor. Mal had kept him up to date with the ongoing shop saga. Chris had seen Nathan's photos of the toys and heard about his suggestion for an exhibition of them inside the shop, to be contained in a set of display cabinets, but the insurance premium required for such valuable items had put paid to that idea. In the end Mrs Cooper had decided to let most of them go, to be sold at a specialist toy auction. The funds raised from the sale had been outstanding and enough for her to set up her dream of a small café-cum-bookshop. Nathan had made large posters and framed pictures of all the toys to decorate the counter area. Then to add to the intertest he had set up a stock of postcards of them, which she could also sell in the shop. Chris was delighted to know how well this had all turned out, and that Mal and Nathan had gone out of their way to prove their caring nature. The world needed more people like them.

Chris was also quite happy with his next task. He had been sent to interview a businessman about his project in the inner city, to promote and encourage the youngsters to form a community choir. Morris Derrick had in the past achieved a similar success in other run-down parts of cities. He would find unwanted empty buildings he could use and have volunteers make them fit for habitation, providing a base for the choirs to rehearse in.

Chris instantly warmed to the man and was impressed by his genuine enthusiasm to inspire the youngsters to help them improve themselves. He wrote a very good article and smiled when he saw it in print. He had every confidence it would promote interest in Morris's dedicated approach. The man could do with extra backing. There were days when Chris actually loved his work.

The next week, by contrast, the editor had made a change in Chris's schedule and he was stuck with one of the most boring interviews in a long time. He walked back into the news office afterwards, flopped into his chair and closed his eyes to recoup his energy. It had been draining to listen to the droning, flat dull tone of someone who never stopped talking. Trust his voice recorder to be on the blink. He had had to make notes by hand, and his wrist hurt. Goodness knows what he could find in it that was worth using.

He wiggled his shoulders and stretched his neck in a circle. Then he immersed himself back in trying to sort out his notes. All this effort for what would only be a fill-in piece of a couple of columns to meet tonight's deadline. It seemed totally stupid to him.

The only thing to perk him up had been some glossy brochures he had picked up earlier in the day. He had been passing through a foyer when he spotted a poster about a forthcoming auction in the hotel, of prime location property in the capital. He took a look at the brochure. The photos were stunning and the interiors were high class, state-of-the-art designs. How the other half lived! He picked up a couple of the brochures for his sisters, knowing that they would appreciate them.

His copy complete and ready to go home, Chris became aware of a growing uproar in the main newsroom. The reporters were calling out to each other whilst tapping away like mad on their keyboards. The phones were in full use as the staff were desperate to get international calls to Paris, to get hold of developing information. Apparently, there had been a multiple terrorist attack on three sites in the city.

It made everyone shiver. No one had quite forgotten the awful attack in January on a weekly newspaper, the *Charlie Hebdo*. The atmosphere was strained, and the editors and sub-editors were reading everything as it was written. The front page and the headlines were being altered every few minutes as the deadline approached. The manic effort to capture the terrible events showed on their faces. The news never changed; good or bad, it had to be printed.

One evening in the lead up to Christmas, Callum phoned

Chris. His term work done, he dejectedly complained that he almost dreaded going home for the holidays, but he mentioned that on returning home, he meant to visit the attic, to see what Rosie had kept up there. Why shouldn't he? It was not her exclusive domain. The thought of her toys in the attic, and the sketchbook he had never seen, irritated him. Tactfully Chris refrained from either encouraging him or dissuading him. Maybe that was exactly what needed to be done, Chris thought, but he did not say it aloud.

Whilst Matt and his brother were with their family over the festive season, Chris and Bridget spent Christmas Day and Boxing Day with Paula, Ray and their two sons. The usual chaos reigned as they shared the traditional old-fashioned Christmas; the house decorated from top to bottom, the wrapping paper and presents strewn around the tree, the roast dinner, walks and games involving everyone in the afternoon, a late tea, more games, singing Christmas songs, noise and laugher, and a supper of cheese, pickle and cold meat. All of which was repeated on a smaller scale the next day, because they were shattered.

The day after Boxing Day, a very chipper Callum phoned Chris to let him know he had had the best Christmas ever. He hadn't needed to search the loft space. Out of the blue Rosie had actually dragged him into the loft, where she had cleared a space and laid her sketchbook on the top of her toy box for him. She had allowed him to linger over her treasured pictures.

"I don't know what made her have a change of heart," he said. "Honestly Chris, I could not have been happier, I really couldn't. It felt like we were friends again. It was worth the wait."

Still no mention of Jake, Chris noticed. Although knowing about him, Callum had decided not to force the issue. He would let Rosie be. Their friendship depended on it.

"As it is, Rosie is thinking of inviting Bridget up in early January for the big New Year craft fair in the grounds of Aston Hall. She has suggested the four of us could go together. Please say you can come up."

In early January, at Rosie's suggestion, Chris and Bridget went up for the weekend so that the four of them could go to the Winter Craft Fair. They both knew from Callum that there had been a breakthrough. Rosie's unexpected change of heart had surprised them. Had the talking they had done with her at half-term done the trick? It looked promising. They were pleased that Callum would be included in their day out. They asked Aunt Mary to join them, but she was much too sensible to agree to be out in the cold for that length of time.

As expected the girls went off around the stalls, leaving the boys to make their own way around the fair. Naturally Callum and Chris had soon had enough of the market and went off into the grounds instead. Callum had not explored the gardens on their first visit, but this time he kept stopping and staring around. He frowned slightly and looked at Chris.

"I can't quite believe this," he said. He explained that he could recognise certain views from Rosie's drawings: the topiary, the steps from the main drive down through the box hedge designs, the archway through to the kitchen garden and the shapes of the hills beyond the lower fence were all familiar. He even recognised the solitary tree in the corner of the field at the far end just before the wood started. He had never realised how accurate her simple sketches had been until now, looking at the original views. Jake's death had a lot to answer for. All that talent wasted.

When the four of them met up again, Rosie made no qualms about going off for a few private moments on her own, while the rest of them went for a hot drink in the café. There a happier Callum seemed resigned to the fact that despite Rosie's change of heart over the drawings, she had still refused to talk about Jake. Sadly, he accepted that the subject would remain off limits. Her silent devotion to his memory would always be there inside her, locked away and cherished forever. That was his only disappointment, the one slight shadow between them. But he would have to live with it, to accept that life is like that and make the best of what they had. Chris had never heard such wisdom from his younger cousin before; it was a good sign.

They continued to mull over other topics for another half hour as they waited for Rosie to reappear. What had happened to her? It was turning cold and the place would soon close. As the others went back to the car, Chris set off to the kitchen garden, expecting to find her there, but she wasn't and he was forced to do a quick search around the place. Finally, as the mist was softening the view into a mystical landscape, he saw her down by the big old oak tree beyond the formal gardens. This must have been where Jake died, because as he watched she gently touched the wrinkled bark and gently kissed it. Then, her private act of remembrance over, she calmly turned to walk back towards the main buildings.

Chris quickly stepped back out of sight. He took a different route back before intercepting her as if by accident just as she arrived back in the courtyard.

"It's beautiful to see the gardens in all the different seasons," she said, smiling. There was nothing sad in her manner. While the subject of Jake might be off limits to others, Chris felt he had the benefit of inside knowledge which allowed him to ask questions.

"What happened to the tin box you wanted to give to Jake when he died? Jake's grandfather told me about it when I first met him."

He saw her stiffen, then smile.

"He seems to have told you quite a lot. I buried it by the tree."

"What was in it?" Chris asked quietly.

"A message for Jake," she whispered.

Chris nodded and patted her hand understandingly. She responded by tucking her arm in his to walk alongside him.

"I hear you've shown Callum your drawings recently," said Chris. "Well done. I think he needed that."

They returned to the car in silence.

"What's it like inside the big house?" Bridget asked Rosie on the way home.

"We were never allowed in it. The strict owner never let anyone invade his private quarters."

"I would love to have a look inside when it's open to the public again."

Rosie pulled a face. "I don't know why. It is only some boring old building."

"Dark, dull and dusty, like all the rest," Chris joked, remembering their childhood coach trips, when they had been dragged round numerous period houses.

From the front of the car Callum studied Rosie hard via the mirror. Her lack of interest in the main house made him frown. Once home, Callum stopped Chris from following the girls inside.

"There's something I want to check out," he whispered. "Make sure you stay behind tomorrow morning."

Bridget had already bought many weird and wonderful items to add to her work collection, but she intended to go shopping in Cambridge as well. No sooner had she and Rosie taken Aunt Mary out the next morning than Callum took Chris up into the attic. He had never spent time there before and was eager to take the chance to have a good look around. The little skylight threw thin rays of light over the room, which was filled with all kinds of family jumble; carpets, rugs, boxes and shelves of knick-knacks, an old sewing machine, suitcases, a train set and childhood furniture. It was a haven of memories to explore, but he was not here for that. He soon noticed Rosie's precious belongings, the old travelling trunk and toys, all wrapped in plastic sheeting and gathering dust.

Callum moved boxes to make two makeshift seats and a larger flat surface to act as a table top. Then he spread out Rosie's sketch book and slowly turned the pages, letting Chris see for himself the scenes of the grounds Rosie had so delicately drawn. They were beautiful. Chris could not help thinking how miffed Bridget would be to know she had missed this treat. Not that he could dare to tell her until they were home. He had to agree with his cousin that the views were instantly recognisable. What was more, they were drawn in sequence as she moved from viewpoint to viewpoint around the grounds. You could almost plot her route.

He flipped through the pages until, at the back of the book, he came to a contradiction. Every view had been drawn from outside, except the last, which was obviously an interior view of the main house.

"What do you think?" said Callum. "This one is so out of place. Why would Rosie have drawn this scene? And why make out she had never been inside?"

"She didn't actually say she had not been in the house, only that they were not allowed inside."

"Hmm. Well, I'm sure she was prevaricating about that. I think the interior is important to her for some reason."

"Or you could be making something out of nothing," Chris suggested. He was not convinced by the notion his cousin had raised. All that mattered was that if Callum had not come up with this crazy idea, Chris would never have got to see these lovely drawings for himself.

Replacing the book and all the boxes in their original places, they returned to the kitchen. But Callum was not going to give up that easily. After his cousins had left for home and Rosie and his aunt had gone out, he was back up in the attic like lightning to study the pictures again. That last picture of the interior intrigued him. He was not convinced Chris was right to ignore it, but he could hardly tackle Rosie about it without causing more trouble.

Chris shared Callum's remarks about the last drawing to Bridget once they were home, to get her take on the matter. She did not see it as a mystery either and agreed that it did not warrant further consideration. As a former art student, she had drawn anything and everything, just because she could. There was no pattern to the pictures which had covered the walls of their old home, she reflected. Yes, Chris could vouch for that. All that paper and coloured paint, scissors and glue. She made a mess everywhere. Every spare cupboard had been full of her junk, no one else got a look in, he teased, ducking quickly out of reach of the expected playful thump.

The rough and tumble of their childhood had made them what they were. He would not have changed it for anything. They had been lucky to have shared so much. With Callum and Rosie friends again, and Bridget and Matt closer than ever, Chris considered there was little to worry about any more.

CHAPTER 7

In the New Year Chris continued to report on the various news items which cropped up, and January was marked by the passing of several popular favourite icons, which touched the public in general: the actor Alan Rickman, the musician David Bowie and that most treasured radio and television personality Terry Wogan. It was hard to imagine Terry's beloved voice and humour had gone from them. It felt like everyone had lost a friend.

In February the rumour that the *Independent* and the *Independent on Sunday* had been sold to Johnston Press and would be on line only in future sent a worrying signal to the newspaper industry. Chris and Stan and Ron, his regular rival acquaintances, plus Freddie from the *Mail*, exchanged grimaces and shook their heads. All were concerned about the encroaching social media technology which threatened their livelihoods. They could only battle on. It was what these well-seasoned newsmen had learnt to do.

Chris marched angrily around the *Despatch* newsroom. He would not be ground down by the expanding technology or these wayward interlopers. No one was going to change the way he did his job. It worked. He had a good system and he was good at his job. No one could deny that.

A few days later, he attended a reception as a favour for a colleague. After recording the important issues during the speeches and dinner, he left the complex to look for the nearest bar. He needed a drink. On his way through the hotel foyer, a short cut he often used, he stopped abruptly. A man he thought he would never see again, that Italian charmer from Sardinia, had entered through the main door. There was no mistaking him. The man beamed at the receptionist, just as he had done in Pula, and thanked her for ordering the theatre tickets. His family followed him in, his beautiful wife clothed in a distinctive designer outfit, with a very expensive grey fur wrap draped around her shoulders and the children equally well attired. They were the picture of an elite society family after a night out.

Chris stood there watching them, his mouth open. What was he doing here? A family holiday? Possibly, but he could not ignore the question which was burning in his mind. Had Savante come to London intending to see Francesca again?

Was this really a coincidence? But why should he jump to that conclusion simply because she was working in London at the same time?

He walked through the city streets, trying to control the niggling suspicion building inside him. How long was Savante staying? He hated the idea that Francesca was still involved with this married man. Their relationship must have fizzled out by now; she had built an important career at the hotel. She would not risk ruining her future. Why could he not stop thinking about it? But he could not shake it from his mind. He knew he had to do something constructive to shake of his obsession, and he had the answer. The only way to calm himself down was to spend time investigating the man, for no particular reason except to would give him some satisfaction. He would find out everything he could about Olivier Marco Savante, his entire history, the smallest detail, every flaw. He knew he should not, but he was so angry that he could not help himself. He already knew the man's name. He would check the office database. Tonight.

Chris had always thrived on the investigative side of his work and searching for connections. It gave him a buzz. It was something he revelled in. Tonight was no exception.

"What the devil are you doing?" Cherry asked out of nowhere. He had not heard her come into the office.

"Something private" he mumbled, hoping she had not seen the data on the computer screen before he quickly closed the page.

Cherry collected her bag, reminded him how late it was and left.

Chris waited until he heard the outer security door slam before resuming his research. Unfortunately, it did not take long to discover there was hardly anything to find. The limited information had Savante listed as a wealthy businessman, a man of property and little else. He printed off a few details and studied them before phoning one or two of his contacts. They were able to add nothing.

He was coming to the conclusion that he would need to scour the internet in Italian, and that meant trying to coerce Cherry into helping him, because her Italian was fluent. That was going to be tricky.

The next morning he bought Cherry a coffee and began trying to persuade her to help him, admitting that it was nothing to do with work and he would consider it a personal favour. He simply wanted to get some background data.

"Why?" Cherry asked. "If it isn't connected to a story, why you are bothering?"

"I saw someone I never expected to see here, in London. It made me curious."

"Curious?"

"I thought he might have a dubious background."

"God help the rest of the world then, if you intend to investigate everyone who crosses your radar."

She stopped what she was doing and sat back, arms folded, to look at Chris. Obviously, she was already suspicious of his agenda. He could hardly tell her of Francesca's involvement with this man. It was better to say nothing. Cherry huffed and puffed, but as a friend she begrudgingly delved into the Italian records for him.

The results were disappointing. Oliviero Savante turned out to be one of the most influential and respected men in Florence and was quietly worshipped by half of Italian society. The man was a demigod, independently wealthy and a director of a host of private companies. His earlier reputation as one of the most eligible bachelors had linked him with several famous and beautiful women, but by all accounts he was now a happily married man, devoted to his wife and children. Nowhere in his past was there a hint of any scandal.

This was not the information Chris wanted. While Cherry searched for anything new, he scanned several other brief biographies he found in English, discovering that the Savante family spent every summer in Sardinia. It was no secret. If he had ever done anything wrong, it had never appeared in print.

"What do you intend to do with all this?" Cherry asked as she picked up her bag to leave.

"Stick it in a drawer for now."

Cherry shook her head and banged the office door loudly behind her. She felt sure that Chris had wasted his time and hers, for no good reason.

In the office again a few days later, Chris took the papers

out of the drawer and re-read the contents of the dossier he had begun on the Italian. Nothing could placate his niggling irritation that the man was here in London. He decided to scribble down some notes about his holiday sightings of Francesca and Savante. He did not want to forget anything which might make sense later. He shuffled the pages together and sat staring at them, logic trying to win over speculation. The fact that Savante was in London meant nothing. The fact that he had seen them together in Sardinia last summer did not mean their association had resumed. And yet…

"I thought you had stopped this," Cherry snapped at him from behind. "I hope you're not trying to crucify the man for no good reason."

"I can't help being inquisitive."

"Inquisitive! It's beginning to look more like a fixation. What is it you are not telling me?"

She snatched the papers away from him and keeping her distance, quickly scanned the handwritten contents. She fully understood the implication of his account and turned back to face him, glaring fiercely. He had never seen her so angry, her jaw fixed and face full of fury. Thank goodness there was no one else in the office.

"I can't believe you. How dare you speculate about their private life. It is none of your concern."

"It is only my personal observations."

"Then keep them to yourself, out of the office. If this woman wants to see this man, I am sure she knows precisely what she is doing. If she's an astute businesswoman, I doubt she is anybody's fool. I am sure she can look after herself."

Chris cleared his throat and diverted his eyes to the floor. No doubt she could.

"Anyone can get hurt," he mumbled in his defence.

"And so will you, if you don't stop this now!" She gave him a sharp clip around the shoulders and threw the papers back on his desk so that they scattered everywhere.

Chris gathered them up, pushed them into an envelope and threw them into his desk drawer. Then he copied the dossier files from his office computer to his personal flash drive before irreversibly deleting them from the public domain. He had to admit that he was losing his professional impartiality. God, Ellen would never have allowed him to do this. She would have stopped him. She would be ashamed of him. Ellen had been his conscience. What was wrong with him? He should have known better, he should forget about it. He had other things to deal with. He promised himself he would shred the papers later.

That evening Chris was trying to put his mind in order when Ray phoned him, something which was highly unusual.

"What's up?" was his instant response.

"Nothing. How are Bridget and Matt getting on these days?"

Chris frowned at the phone. Why was Ray, not Paula, checking up?

"I have no idea. Why?"

"I'm only teasing. It's the boys. When they got a look

at Matt from the window when he called in with Bridget recently, they started turning out their old sports magazines."

"So?"

"They are convinced he used to be a famous rugby player."

Ray was wondering whether he should clarify their suspicions or if it was best left alone.

"I'm sure Bridget has no idea, otherwise she would have said something," he said. "I hope he isn't famous, otherwise it's going to be difficult to control them."

Chris raised his eyebrows and shrugged. He was all for leaving things alone. He had already tried to gain a clearer impression of Matt over the past months and had been getting nowhere fast. He had searched Google for any recent accidents connected to his name and found nothing at all. He guessed it might not have been newsworthy enough. Although curious about Matt's aversion to the press initially, he had dismissed it as just a private viewpoint. Everyone had their views, and the press did not always do themselves any favours. Then there were other puzzles he had not solved. He had always felt that it was odd that Mike, as a police officer, could manage so much compassionate leave to take care of Matt. Then again, had Matt avoided the public for another reason, not because he was on crutches or the difficulty of walking? Was it because he did not want to be seen at all or recognised? But why? What was behind this odd behaviour? He hadn't fully appreciated what Matt had done for a living. Did Bridget?

Then he shook himself free of all this additional ridiculous theorizing. This was stupid! He was doing it again. Francesca and Olivier one day and now Matt. He could not help letting his imagination run away with such unsubstantiated ideas. Yet he had always been highly sceptical in his job; it was in his nature.

The next day Chris decided to contact his older sister, to try some indirect sleuthing.

"Oh, Paula. I'm sorry to phone, but I wondered what you thought of Matt, now you have met him properly?" There was no point in admitting his suspicions.

"Chris, you needn't worry. I'm sure he's a good man. Bridget is happy, and it's going so well. Oh, hang on. Ray's making faces, he wants to talk to you, here you are."

"Er – Hi Chris. I need to talk to you. Wait. I'll just let Paula go back into the other room."

There was a pause before he continued.

"I didn't want Paula to hear this. I'm not sure where to start. First off, do you remember I told you about the boys finding those old sports magazines? They've been bending my ear ever since. The boys are still adamant that Matt is Matt Hiller. They're not going to let it go. Plus they keep on asking when he's coming again. They are desperate to meet him. They are sure it's him, despite the beard. Apparently his career ended after an accident."

Chris felt the whole idea was ridiculous. How would Bridget have met a famous sportsman? Certainly not in a car park in the middle of nowhere, as she had. That would be too bizarre.

"All right, we know Matt was injured, but the rest can't be right."

"The problem is I don't think Bridget knows everything about him. Look anyway. Paula is already complaining that she finds it peculiar that our sons are so interested in him. Although the boys might have promised to keep quiet for the moment, I don't hold out much hope of that lasting forever. Children are unreliable. They are dying to tell their friends what they have found out."

It was obvious to Ray that he would not be able to keep this secret much longer. He needed an ally who could ease the situation, he explained – Chris.

Chris did not quite understand how he was supposed to help, until Ray explained.

"The point is, I think Bridget should be told before Paula finds out from our sons and tells her. I think you should be the one to tell her."

"Tell her what exactly? I don't know anything."

"Because you would be better handling this. Listen, I suggest you to talk to your sports desk tomorrow. Then you can decide how much to tell her. It could be quite enlightening."

"Sports desk? Rugby? Ray! For goodness sake, tell me."

His brother-in-law laughed at the other end of the phone.

"Calm down. It's not that bad."

"How bad then?"

"You're the investigative reporter. I'm not going to do all the work for you."

Ray put the phone down, leaving Chris to ponder. As if he was going to wait until tomorrow! He logged into the internet on his laptop and this time he typed in Matt's name and 'rugby'. There was nothing. Strange… His fingers drummed on the desk top as he wondered what else to look up.

His mind was on overdrive as he sank into his chair, his coffee growing cold and his toast only half eaten beside him. He could only wonder at what the next day would turn up.

The next morning Chris was in the *Despatch* newsroom early and made his way straight to the sports department, to be met by Harry, the very sceptical sports editor.

"What on earth are you doing coming in here? You hate sport," was the off-hand greeting.

"Do you know anything about a rugby player called Matt Hiller?"

"And why would you want to know?"

Chris could see Harry was being deliberately pedantic and enjoying the situation. No doubt payback for Chris having banned his staff from popping in to see Alan.

"Does it matter?"

"That depends. I don't want you interviewing our sporting personalities."

"For goodness' sake, I wouldn't dare. Are you going to help or not?"

Chris was getting fed up with this game, but then Harry relented and typed 'Matt Hiller' into the website search facility. It drew a blank. No matches were found. Something was wrong. Ray had been so positive that the newspaper would have all the information he needed about Matt.

"I tried putting his name into Google last night, but nothing came up. He may just be a club player, but I thought I would check it out with you."

The smirk on Harry's face indicated that he had something up his sleeve, something he was keeping back.

"Of course it might help if you had the correct surname. Matt *Hillier* would be a different story."

Hardly had the new name been entered than an entire sports career appeared on the screen. It was extensive and impressive.

"There you go, Matt Hillier. He's quite important. Played for England, until his accident."

Chris stared at the monitor. This man was indeed a well-known international rugby player. Ray and the boys were right. He had come from a local club to be being signed up for one of the major London clubs before being picked for the England team. There were a lot of articles praising his skill as a fly half. His direct attacking play and passing talent had him compared to the England star Jonny Wilkinson, since he was also their best goal kicker.

Then there was more. As well as Matt's brilliant rugby history there were stories about his former extravagant London lifestyle and reports of his accident, the event which had ruined his career. A cold shiver ran through him. This was Bridget's boyfriend. This was a nightmare!

"If you had known anything about sport, you could have searched other websites," said Harry. 'Twickenham team members' would have been a good start."

Chris pulled a face, not knowing what to say.

"If you ever come across him, I wouldn't mind an interview."

That seemed unlikely.

Chris returned to his office in a daze and googled Matt Hillier in his own time. Poor Bridget, she had no idea who he was. Ray had made it clear that he considered Chris the most suitable person for the task of breaking the news to her. Someone must warn her, but was it really up to him? This was not fair, but there was no one else. Thanks and no thanks, Ray!

He spent the rest of the morning thinking about the problem whilst attempting to do his normal work. What would be the best way to approach the subject, and how much did he dare to tell her? That he had been famous? No. That he had been part of the English international rugby team? No. That he was a famous celebrity? Certainly not!

It certainly explained Matt's reticence to say much about himself or to appear in public places. If he had been invalided after such great sporting success, it was no wonder he hadn't told Bridget anything. If only he had, Chris would not be facing this awkward task.

Chris arrived on his sister's doorstep the same day having finished work early. He had never felt so unprepared. How do I do this? he kept asking himself. How to keep it simple and not alarm her? He just wanted to get this over with. He hoped it would not all go terribly wrong.

"This is unexpected. I don't usually see you midweek. I thought I was meeting you in town on Friday," Bridget muttered as she let him in.

Chris explained that he had been coming this way and had only dropped in for a coffee. He was not stopping. And yes, they were still on for Friday.

"Ray phoned me the other day," he said.

"Nothing wrong with Paula?" was his sister's instant response.

"No. Everything is fine."

She went back to dicing the vegetables, unconcerned.

"He mentioned something about Matt."

This time Bridget put down the knife and looked at him.

"His name is Matthew Hillier, isn't it?"

She nodded. That was it then. He did not have any excuse to dodge the issue.

"Ray says the boys recognised him. He was a well-known rugby player."

She shrugged, frowned at him briefly and turned back to her chores.

"Even if he was, it hardly makes any difference. It's obviously not important anymore."

Chris drew a breath, aware how carefully he should continue.

"He has never mentioned it?"

She shook her head and smiled. It did not matter what his work had been, he could have been a street cleaner or refuse collector for all she cared. It did not make any difference to the way she felt about him. She was quite happy with the ordinary man he was, she declared.

"You aren't bothered by his sporting past?"

"Why on earth should I be? It's hardly going to impact on our lives. He clearly won't be playing any more. He wants a new career."

Chris could see Bridget did not take his concern seriously. He looked at his lovely bright-eyed sister and made a decision. There was no point in upsetting her. She was quite content with how things were and he was certainly not going to be the one to threaten that happiness. She wasn't one of those people who bought celebrity magazines or read their gossip columns, so why tell her? With any luck her ignorance would be a blessing. Fingers crossed, there was little chance she would find out.

Bridget had been quite happy to brush aside her brother's disclosures. The fact that Matt had not mentioned his sporting career fitted in with his general reluctance to talk about himself. She had accepted his tactful protection of his privacy as part of his character. There was no point in dwelling on it, there was more to their relationship than delving into what he was before. Although certain things were becoming clear. She did remember her nephews' excitement about the prospect of him visiting. Then there were those children in the park who had looked at him in awe. Maybe sportsmen become used to adoration. Maybe he did not like that adoration any more. Still, it would not hurt to tease him about making his past career such a secret.

Matt had learnt not to rush things and the specialist had at last declared him fully fit. The leg was strong enough. The calliper was ditched and he tentatively walked around without the need of the walking stick either. He was being careful and did not push himself too much, as he had learnt his lesson from last time despite feeling better than ever. After a few weeks, he had mastered the old tractor and had driven it round and round the farm, over every bone-shaking bump. He had bought a car and was going to take Bridget to the forthcoming village dance, not that he had told her yet. He had not danced for ages, and he needed to practise his footwork. Thank goodness his parents still had their collection of old dance records. Plus he had a gem of an idea for a future career, but that had to be explored too, before he said anything to anyone.

Matt had been in town at his brother's home, sorting out some of the boxes he had brought over from his own flat, when Bridget phoned to ask him to call in on his way back to his parents. Which he dutifully did. Her twinkling eyes told him she had something to say, but what? She let him settle himself comfortably on the settee before she began.

"Ok, Matt. It's time for a little straight talking," she said. "It is not enough to speak, but to speak true."

Shakespeare again. Matt looked startled; he could not imagine what was coming. He had not done anything wrong, had he?

"Now, will you please tell me what you did previously for a living?"

"I told you before, I had a variety of mundane jobs. It was mainly outside physical work. Nothing special."

"Nothing special? Well, is that right! Really Matt, it is no good you pussyfooting about any more. You are busted, sunshine."

Matt did not speak, wondering what she had found out. If her brother, the journalist, had done some digging, then he would have discovered everything. Had he spilled the beans? If so, he was in for trouble. But Bridget did not look angry.

"My nephews are sports mad, and they're convinced you were a famous rugby player. Are they right? Why didn't you tell me?"

Matt waited for the inevitable conclusion. If she knew about his past, she would not like him any more, but Bridget seemed quite oblivious.

"There was no point in dwelling over it. That career is over. I have to move on. I have to make a fresh start."

This was clearly fine with her, because instead of replying, she simply kissed him. He had been lucky. He wrapped his arms around her and kissed her back. They did not need any more words to fill the comfortable silence between them. The village dance lingered in his mind, but that could wait.

Both Chris and Ray were surprised by Bridget's positive reaction to Matt's revelation. She was very laid back about the whole matter when she spoke to Paula. There had been no fireworks or ranting and raving. Matt had clearly avoided telling her he had been famous. It remained a secret. They couldn't blame the guy for that. Nor could they blame Matt for timing his visits with Bridget to Paula and Ray when the boys were at school. During these visits his career was not mentioned in conversation, which was quite frustrating, as Ray really wanted to hear about it.

Chris realised why he would be the last on the list to meet Matt; it was because he was a member of the press. Matt must dread the idea of intrusive journalists asking about what had happened. Well so be it, Chris didn't mind, now that he understood the reason. Yet it was strange that every mention of rugby now had him thinking of Matt, and also thinking of the accident, which on reflection had him puzzled. His newspaperman's instinct was already questioning why the ensuing television coverage had come up short on facts. There had been little news about it, no police reports or bulletins from the hospital. It was as if the details were being kept from the public. It was obvious now that this wall of silence was designed to hide the real seriousness of the incident. He felt uneasy.

In the office, Cherry complained that she did not hear or see much of Bridget these days. Was she all right? Was she still with that boyfriend?

"Oh, she's fine. They are fine," Chris murmured.

If Cherry expected him to elaborate, she was to be disappointed. He was not about to tell her who this man actually was. He could keep a secret as well as Matt.

Then Alan interrupted to ask Chris if he had seen the latest piece about Morris Derrick in one of the morning tabloids.

"You interviewed him last month. Can you believe any of this?"

He passed Chris the newspaper so he could read the column for himself. The more Chris read, the more indignant he became. Chris was furious. Mr Derrick's reputation was being threatened by vague and unsubstantiated rumours of crooked dealings. Some vicious person was ruining all the hard work Mr Derrick had done to promote interest in the youth choir. Chris did not usually let stories get to him, but this was different. He decided to counter the allegations by writing another piece for the *Despatch* praising the good work the man was doing. The man deserved all the public support he could get.

Left in peace, Chris set to, to write a seething attack on the unscrupulous hacks who gave a bad name to decent journalists. He had to get it out of his system. He did not move until he had finished. Although the editor was unlikely to print such a contentious article about their own profession, he felt much better after venting his feelings through the written word.

A few hours later, the earlier tension seemed nothing compared to the panic he was beginning to feel. Cherry discovered him rummaging amongst the scattered papers covering his desk and littering the floor.

"I can't find them."

"Find what?"

"You know what, my abandoned research stuff on the Italian businessman. I was sure it was all in this drawer. I meant to shred the documents, but I hadn't got around to doing it."

"You've lost them?"

"I haven't, they were here. Did you take them?"

"Me! Why would I take them?"

"Someone must have."

Chris returned to checking the muddle of strewn papers, not daring to take his eyes off of them in case he missed anything.

"For god's sake, will you just help me? You can tell me off when I've found them."

"*If* you find them," Cherry muttered. "You should have never have left them in an open drawer. It's your own fault they are missing. I am appalled at your stupidity. Heavens knows what will happen if anyone else puts that stuff into print."

Chris snarled. It irritated him that Cherry was telling him what he had worked out for himself. He did not need reprimanding by her. He didn't care what Cherry thought of him; finding the incriminating pages was more important than arguing with her. This was a disaster.

"Yes, OK, OK. That's why I want to find them, to make sure they don't."

He sat down and stared at the ceiling, trying to think. He had already mentally acknowledged the damage the disclosure of his holiday observations could do to Francesca, and the aftermath of finding herself splattered across the gossip columns could be a hundred times more dire. He could be in deep trouble, perhaps with legal action against him. It would be the end of his career. Hell, he had never been in such trouble.

"What do I do if I can't find them?"

Cherry let him stew for a while as she slowly strolled around the office. There was only one course open to him, in her opinion. One he would not like.

"You have really gone down in my estimation, Chris Page. You have to face Miss Lawson, you have to warn her, in person. You owe her that. You have to."

Was she mad? He could not think of anything worse. He could not imagine how bad telling Francesca would be. He leaned forward and put his head in his hands, trying to think of a way out of this mess. He could not find one.

No wonder Cherry hated him. He could not forgive himself. He was about to be responsible for a dose of exactly the sort of despicable tittle-tattle he hated. He was worse than the man who had targeted Morris Derrick. That was only inuendo, but his dossier had all the facts. It could appear anywhere, at any time, in any newspaper. How could he prevent it happening? He couldn't. Cherry was right; he was going to have to face Francesca, and warn her.

CHAPTER 8

A very subdued Chris came into work the next day, his mood not helped by the disruption on the Underground because of a drivers' strike. This meant another stressful journey home. He would be glad when it was over.

A few hours later he had composed himself enough to make that difficult call. There was no one else in the office to hear him. With bated breath he phoned the Marriott and asked for Francesca's personal secretary again, to see if he could talk to her or make an appointment. The response scuppered his hopes. He was told that she had been called away for business in France and her diary was full for the rest of the week. She was due back on the Eurostar on Wednesday evening. Two whole days. Two days of agony to wait to see if any of his incriminating conjectures appeared in the media before she returned. Hell! His head was throbbing again.

He asked, pleaded, if she could be persuaded to phone him between meetings. It was urgent, he insisted, and personal, and no, he couldn't leave a message. He would leave his name and phone number. That would be better than nothing.

The Wednesday evening found Chris replacing the receiver thoughtfully as he finished the last of many calls to check train arrival times. When he had the information, he realised his nerves were getting the better of him, and he sat down in the now-empty office to stare out of the window into the wet London night, seeing nothing except his own tired reflection looking back. Who was he? Some pathetic journalist who had to sort out a problem that was all his own fault.

Finally he forced himself to set off for the station. The roads were busy even at that late hour and he cursed the car in front, knowing that at all costs he had to speak to Francesca, but doubting he would get to the station in time.

He struggled to remain alert as he stalked the station concourse. He looked at his watch for the umpteenth time, the minutes barely changing, yet it felt like he'd been there for ages. He had punched the coffee machine enough times to finally learn the knack of actually catching the cup and contents together. A few chocolate bars had done nothing for his hunger, but his determination to see Francesca conquered all discomfort. Face drawn, his eyes darted about as he struggled to see down the platform. His rather odd behaviour caused passing travellers to eye him with suspicion and give him a wide berth.

At last the train's arrival was announced and he held his breath as he watched the small group of passengers filter through the gateway. At first he worried that she would not be there, and then he worried that she would. He was spellbound when she appeared striding down the platform. There was no denying her elegance and air of self-assurance as she strode along the concourse. He swallowed hard and took a determined step forward.

He was greeted by a dark glare and a slight raise of her eyebrows.

"What are you doing here?" she asked, quickly snatching her suitcase away from his offered gesture to carry it.

"I have to talk to you. It's important," he said gruffly.

"I do not appreciate being waylaid out of the blue, Mr Page. If you want another interview, please phone the office."

"It can't wait. I need to talk to you now," he replied. He was hardly going to give up now, after all he had put himself through to be here this evening.

"Stop bothering me!" she insisted, very loudly.

In his peripheral vision, he could see two transport police officers heading in their direction. Heck, he did not need their interference. It could be awkward to explain if they became involved. He did not want a scene.

His hesitation allowed her to quickly march past him and head off through the masses towards the taxi rank and the waiting cars outside. He doggedly pushed through the crowds to catch up with her, knocking and bumping into other people. But every time he managed to move in front of her, she simply side-stepped around him.

"Will you go away? I have a car waiting."

"Please. It is really important."

"Not to me it isn't!" she snapped.

"But it is. It concerns you."

As she slowed by the parked cars, Chris caught her arm to delay her, but before he could do anything else, an imposing driver in uniform, built like a tank, stepped in between them. His menacing presence stopped Chris in his tracks. He had no choice except to back off. Her case was firmly stowed in the boot, and Chris could only watch forlornly as she stepped into a smart limousine and slammed the door. This was hardly the result he had planned. Bloody obstinate woman!

He dragged himself into the office the next morning wondering what to do next. He had hardly read what was on his computer screen when Cherry approached him to hand him a piece of paper. On it was a time and a date. Out of thin air Cherry had miraculously made an appointment with Francesca for him for later that day. How had she managed that? Not that he cared.

He returned to the plush offices of the Marriott Hotel, feeling the same as he had done whilst waiting at the station. Shown into the same office, she indicated for him to sit. He shook his head and remained standing. He did not want to be comfortable or relaxed. He was here to get this over with as quickly as possible.

"I cannot imagine what it is you are here about."

"I have come to apologise in person."

"Apologise for what?"

Chris paused. He could only tell her the situation as it was. No flannel, plain talking. His eloquent, flowing prose was no good here.

"I have some unpleasant news. I did some research on Oliviero Savante after seeing him in London with his family, recently. Notes I have misplaced – lost."

She almost laughed, shaking her head slightly.

"I don't see the problem. His reputation is above reproach. Isn't it?"

"Except I er… did something really stupid. There were more personal observations I made concerning Mr Savante and yourself amongst the papers."

"I beg your pardon?" she said, bristling.

"I saw you together in Sardinia."

"And you thought what?"

He refused to answer. It was better to stay silent. He pushed his tongue into his cheek.

"Your overstretched imagination has a lot to answer for," she snapped.

Francesca stood stony-faced, her eyes narrowed. He waited to be torn to pieces verbally, but the outburst never came. Her cold expression made him shiver. She was too much in control, too calm. He hoped she would listen as he attempted to placate her.

"I meant to destroy them. But it might not be that bad. There is every possibility that even with my notes in the wrong hands, the contents might never come into print."

She scoffed at his stupidity. "You don't really think that, do you?"

"I did try to tell you at the station, but you wouldn't let me."

"It was hardly the place."

"I wanted you to know as soon as possible."

"I accused you last summer of being some scandal-seeking reporter. You convinced me I was wrong. I believed you. That was one hell of a serious mistake on my part. Which will not happen again. Unfortunately, I might not be the only one who has to pay dearly for your unwarranted interest."

"I'm sorry."

"Sorry is hardly good enough. Good day, Mr Page. Security will escort you out of the building."

She buzzed the intercom and issued her instructions, the gist of them being that the gentleman who was leaving was never, ever to be given any future appointments or let into the building again. Chris had not expected anything else.

He left the office. He had said his piece. There was no putting this right. He should never have written anything down. He should have destroyed the notes. How could they have disappeared? The flash drive had gone as well. He could not believe he had mislaid them amongst the mass of other files. How could they have vanished like that? None of his colleagues would stoop so low as to sell information elsewhere for a quick buck. And he could not question everyone in the building without arousing interest in something he wanted kept secret. This did not make sense.

Cherry was less than sympathetic when he gave his account of the meeting on his return to the office.

"Serves you right. That will teach you to be more careful in future."

Yes, he had made a serious mistake. Yes, he felt guilty, but it would be impossible to prevent any revelation eventually appearing in the papers. Although not sensational news, the papers would see it as a way of boosting sales on a quiet day. That was how the media worked.

Alan stepped in to take him for a stiff drink, away from the office. In his opinion, Cherry was not helping matters. "I don't know why she's so hard on you," he said. "It's not as if it's a scoop of national importance, for goodness sake. It is only idle gossip, nothing earth shattering."

After a couple of beers, Chris was almost ready to agree with him. There was nothing he could do. It was out of his hands. He had to stop worrying about it.

But who was he kidding? Chris barely remembered the backgrounds to the tasks he covered over the following days, despite deliberately tackling the most difficult assignments to keep his mind fully occupied. On tenterhooks, he regularly checked the other publications for the stories he dreaded. How long before he could dare to hope that the papers had been lost forever? The only other thing which interrupted his thoughts from time to time was the worry that he had now made a complete hash of his career. He was not the journalist he was.

At the next press conference, where like the rest of the newspaper world he was covering the ongoing EU referendum campaign, he chatted to fellow reporters. He was shocked when Stan mentioned that Ron, a rival fellow-journalist, had quit the profession and was retiring to Suffolk. Ron was sick of the constant boring debates and hated politics. Many others felt the same, but it was part of their responsibility to inform the public. They could not all just turn their back on the news, however boring it was.

Chris had been sent to dig out a human-interest angle on a legal controversy at a period mews complex. With no tenants on site, he did not hope for much. He had tried contacting the council for names, but had got nowhere. If nothing else he would have to find a site manager or land agent and arrange to have a look around.

Set in a narrow, cobbled street, the buildings were empty, boarded up and fenced off. There was no one around to talk to. He decided to try a small shop down the road to ask if anyone local knew the buildings. The woman's shopkeeper's answer perked him up: "Yes, I used to live here."

"I'm doing a piece for the *Despatch*. Would you mind if we had a chat over a hot drink at the corner café when you close for lunch?"

She had no objection and they were soon settled inside, discussing what had happened to the mews complex. She insisted the owner had been a good, considerate landlord, coming down from his home every month to check on the tenants and sort out any problems. They had been lovely homes. Then about ten years ago he had suddenly gone abroad, and it had not been the same since. Even the fine art gallery he owned in Knightsbridge had closed down. Now that he had died overseas, the whole of this property was in litigation, with nothing being done to the buildings until it was sorted out. The tenants had been advised to move out, since there was no caretaker agent to take over the running of the place.

Chris shoved his notebook into his pocket and returned to the office. He typed up what he had and settled down to check the internet for anything else he could use. He suddenly realised the owner of these buildings had the same name as the owner of Aston Hall – Captain Tapley. Could it be the same man? He checked the British Newspaper Archive site, to discover he was indeed the same man who had lived at and owned Aston Hall years ago. Well, He didn't have much to start with, but now he could pad the story out a little more.

He could have tried to contact Jake's grandfather for more material, since he was the only one still working there who might have known the owner, but in the end he could not be bothered. He was already fed up with this article. He would use an abridged version of the man's biography, mentioning Aston Hall, the fine art gallery and what had happened to the mews. Then a few comments explaining the difficulty of those tenants wanting to return to their former homes. But even as Chris wrote up his piece, he was far from satisfied with it. It did not meet the standard he set himself and lacked interesting content. In fact, in his own estimation it hardly deserved to be published. Oh well, on to the next job.

Matt was happy that Bridget had asked no more questions. She had met his parents and no one had mentioned rugby. She was coming down to the village dance and staying overnight at the farm. How great was that.

The village dance had been an exhilarating evening in every respect. Here he was on home ground, and the locals made no fuss, as he was still one of them. Everyone knew him and was pleased to see him there. They smiled and chatted about local matters.

Uncle Jim introduced himself to Bridget, since Matt had failed to do so. He had been busy fending off several inquisitive neighbours, which allowed Jim and others to claim a dance with Bridget. She had not minded being sociable and accepted their friendliness in good humour, but was glad to be rescued occasionally.

The idea had been that they had come to dance together, and Matt soon had that sorted. No one else was going to get a look in. He whirled her around in his arms for the rest of the evening until they were both glowing. All that practising under his mother's supervision had paid off. He could not stop smiling.

In fact Matt was feeling more alive with every day that passed. Untapped energy surged through his veins. He was going back to the local aerodrome to sign up for a refresher course in flying light aircraft. He longed to go flying again, to soar in the sky, to experience the thrill of diving through the clouds, the twists and turns over the vast rolling landscape. He was hungry for it. He had not realised how hungry.

Of course, his brother Mike saw this improved mood as a chance to get Matt to deal with the last hurdle. He turned the music down, took the remote control from him, and demanded his attention.

"About the team..."

"No, don't you dare!" Matt snapped. He glared at his brother, his jaw clenched, his eyes narrowed angrily. Matt knew exactly what Mike had in mind. He did not want to see his former team mates. He could not stand the idea of having to endure their well-meant company. Matt did not want their sympathy, pity and supposed understanding, or their over-cheerfulness to compensate for his lack of conversation.

"Matt! Just because you won't see them it doesn't mean

they have given up on you. They still phone me to see how you are."

Matt wanted him to stop, but Mike was determined to launch into the lecture which was long, long overdue. There were times when he wanted to shake his brother for his stubbornness, to make him more reasonable. All right, he could only admire his courage for all he had endured, bur the rest of them had lived through seeing his injuries as well. They had all seen the horrifying wound with the bones exposed through the skin. Hadn't they waited anxiously at the hospital with the family? Hadn't they all been stunned? They had all understood what an open fracture was, but the serious diagnosis the surgeons had given had shocked them: traumatic, comminuted, displaced, unstable fractures requiring an open reduction and internal fixation. They had all been aware that the shattered bones with the swelling and bruising of adjacent structure would damage bone tissues, nerves, muscles and blood vessels, with other complications of infection. There would be no quick fix. They had all been left without words.

"Have you ever thought about them and how bad they feel? They still blame themselves for something they couldn't prevent. None of them were the same afterwards, they changed too. They deserve some consideration."

Matt had no intention of considering how his family and friends felt, because there was a more serious niggle which was eating away at him, selfish and irrational. He had tried to tell himself he should not feel this way and tried to bury it, but it would not go away. How could there be the same camaraderie between them, his best friends and team mates, when he felt cheated of his share of their glory, their success and their victories? It did not help that the English rugby team had just won the Six Nations Grand Slam. It was on the television, in all the papers. He could not avoid seeing their proud faces. It did not help his resentment. No, he couldn't face them.

"You have to talk to them sometime, Matt."

Matt shook his head. He could not imagine that happening.

Callum came to London for an interview after the Easter break, and Chris was providing free board and lodging for the night. Naturally the conversation centred on his prospects after university. A lot depended on his final exams. He wanted to travel, work abroad and make a good career move. He thought of going to Canada, as many of his friends had already moved there. The prospect sounded inviting. Callum felt very positive about his future.

Eventually their conversation returned to Rosie and home. Chris was disappointed to learn that the subject of Jake had remained taboo.

"I tried to make allowances, but it's not the same," said Callum. Chris raised his eyebrows questioningly. He had felt that it had always seemed perfectly natural that Rosie was bound to the grandfather, because of their connection to Jake. But after all these months, her continual visits to

Aston Hall made him wonder if there was more to it. And on his journey home after seeing Callum off on the train, he reflected upon his part in this family's predicament. He had initially been pleased to have reunited Rosie with her grandfather, but he hadn't bargained for the upset it would later cause. Rosie had invaded his head again. Chris wondered how often she visited the tree where Jake had died.

Back at work, Alan asked who wanted to cover the book launch on Thursday, at the Royal Garden Hotel. Chris checked his schedules; he had a slot free and volunteered.

The rest of the week followed the usual pattern, with a variety of assignments keeping him occupied. On the Thursday he had duly attended the book launch in the posh conference room. It was the usual type of event, to publicise a series of children's books. A few speeches were followed by some book signing, with posters and flyers being handed out all over the place. There was a lot of small talk, social chit chat and shaking hands with the press, TV and a few minor celebrities amongst the throng, together with drinks and an elaborate buffet. The publishers had certainly pulled out all the stops to promote the books. Chris secretly admired novelists; he loved books, he loved their imagination. Books could transport you anywhere.

He made a few notes and put his voice recorder back in his pocket. Nathan, his photographer, left and Chris headed for some free food, scanning the room. He doubted his few words would be of any consequence. At least it would not take long to type up his views on the press release, then he could head home. One more day of the same, he reflected.

He had intended to cook that evening, but after the frozen peas bag split, spilling them all over the kitchen floor, he went off the idea. As he swept them up, he decided to settle for something on toast, then to sit down on the settee and not move. It was safer.

He turned the television on, found a recording he had not seen and settled back, but the film was rubbish, and he soon deleted it. Returning to the main station, he found himself watching a travel programme which included many famous English period houses and gardens. This resurrected his memories of Aston Hall, and Rosie. Poor Rosie, it was such a shame her friend Jake had died. It had altered everything. Jake and Rosie were inseparable as children. Chris could only wonder why Jake had been here on his own. Why would he climb the tree anyway? Because he was a child; he didn't need a reason. Then, from nowhere, the dark side of his mind was suddenly questioning why Jake had fallen out of the old tree. No doubt he was well used to climbing, so such a slip seemed strange.

His journey to work the next day seemed to echo the same vague disquiet. There had been more delays on the tube and he was splashed by cars going through puddles as he hurried from the underground station. He was not feeling very sociable as he walked into the office.

His routine began with methodically checking his schedule for the days ahead, but today he found his attention drifting. He had begun to write notes on his story when he found he had stopped mid-page. Poised with pen still in hand, he came to with a start. He had been in that vacant space again. What was bothering him? Why wouldn't his brain function? Because he did not want to face the awful suspicions of last night. Yet he was beginning to think the impossible. Why did he think the worst? The problem was that he could not ignore matters which did not make sense. His inquisitive nature was difficult to rein back.

His strange mood was evident to Cherry, who told him directly what she thought. "You think too much. You can't switch off at times. You need another holiday."

"Where do you suggest this time? Alaska? Is that far enough away from trouble?"

It was Cherry who had recommended Sardinia last year, although it was not her fault he had encountered Francesca.

Then they were both distracted as Alan entered the office, after receiving a ferocious rollicking from their editor. Alan was fuming. He had been blamed for the terrible performance of the junior reporter who had accompanied him that morning. Gerry had given them both a full-blown ear-bashing.

"Thank God they didn't put him in this office," he raged. "I would have strangled him by now. He wouldn't have lasted five minutes. The boy's a fool. They come straight out of college with no idea about people skills. His questions were irrelevant and completely baffling. His copy was rubbish. He made me so angry that I need a drink to calm down."

"Any excuse," said Cherry with a smile.

Alan soon had his low opinion of the younger generation confirmed again. He had had a foreign student renting his late mother's old terrace home, and the man had vacated his lodgings and gone home, leaving the place an untidy mess. He hadn't really expected anything else, but it had come to the point where he had decided to clear the place and sell up. It was too much of a hassle to continue with all the paperwork and regulations, which seemed to get more complicated every year. He wanted to empty the rubbish out before it went on the market, and he was relying on Chris to help him.

Having previously offered in a rash moment to help Alan at any time, Chris now found himself obliged to make good his kind promise. He did not really mind. A bit of physical work would do him good for a change. Besides it would put off the business of painting the bathroom at home for another week. The paint tins were getting dusty and the rest of the paraphernalia piled against the wall seemed to be a permanent feature, one he was quite getting used to. Why disturb them?

Chris had planned a peaceful weekend, and the regular get-together with Tom and Mal. Goodness knows what they would be doing this time. Last month they had had the madcap idea of trying ten-pin bowling. They would not be doing that again. Another outing had seen them standing out in the cold and wind, watching banger racing in a muddy field. There was no rhyme or reason to their social outings, which usually ended with a drink in the nearest hostelry. Sometimes they would just go for a meal. Whatever, it was would be fine.

The next weekend brought a refreshing change. Paula had come up to town to go to a period costume presentation at the V and A Museum with Bridget. Full of girlie talk, they spent most of the day at the exhibition and were both exhausted by the time they met up with Chris at his home. It was the family catch-up time for all three of them, something they had not managed for ages. They laughed a lot and remembered many silly things as they reminisced about their childhood. It was a real treat.

After Paula had left to catch her train, Bridget and Chris sat back to get their breath back. All that talking had made them dry and thirsty and Chris went to make another pot of tea. He would have offered Bridget some wine, but she was driving.

"Has Matt any idea what he wants to do yet?" he asked.

"No, nothing specific. He has signed up for several mechanical courses. As long as he's happy."

She went on to tell him how much she had enjoyed the dance and the weekend at the farm.

"His parents are lovely down-to-earth people. I can see where he gets his determination from."

"Does he miss being in London?"

"Apparently not, he never refers to it. I wish…"

"What?"

"I don't know. Sometimes I get the impression he had more to tell me about himself, but he doesn't. Maybe I'm wrong. Is there anything more you know about Matt?"

"Not a lot. But I would like to meet him. You don't have to keep him all to yourself."

It was a good attempt to defuse the topic, but she ignored his teasing. "Are you sure?"

Chris was prepared to lie, and did so. Bridget was still oblivious to the full picture regarding Matt. Long may it continue.

Another week in the office began, and Chris flicked through the possible events worth covering for the paper. A Metropolitan conference to be held soon caught his attention. He fleetingly thought of volunteering and then sensibly talked himself out of it. He briefly wondered if Matt's brother Mike would be there. He seemed to be back on regular duties now Matt had recovered. He had fulfilled his duty as his brother's supporter and protector, but Chris was still left wondering why it had been necessary. He would have liked to have spoken to Mike. What was the chance of that? A police officer being approached by a stranger, showing his press card as ID, would not be a good move.

During a lull in the lunch hour, the conversation turned to the new style of journalism which was giving the profession a bad name. The illegal hacking of prominent people's phones had become commonplace. The hatchet job on Morris Derrick still angered Chris, who had been to see him soon after the article had been published. He felt he had to apologise and express his regret over it. Few people had sufficient funds for a lengthy legal action to regain one's reputation. After being dragged through the justice system, it was often not worth it, just for a half-hearted retraction or some meagre monetary recompense. Derrick had been quite philosophical and resigned to what had happened. Logically he accepted that he could only struggle on and start again. Chris could only admire his stoicism.

Alan had looked at the forthcoming events they should attend. There were some corkers on the list. Who was going to get best pickings?

"The Marriott is holding a gala charity event next month. Do you want to cover it, Chris?"

Grief, what an idea! The Marriott meant Francesca, and Chris had no doubt his name would be on a black list to make sure he was banned from entering. He wasn't taking any chances. He must surely be persona non grata there.

"Not really. Let Cherry have the pleasure."

Cherry smiled. This was a definite perk. It would be a posh affair. She could dress up in her finest. Did she have a smart enough frock? She was pleased that Chris had turned it down. The run-in with Miss Lawson had proved a blessing after all. *Thank you Francesca*, she whispered to herself.

"Best take a photographer when you go. Pictures of the famous are always a good seller. Report who is there and get the gist of the speeches."

"Any message for Francesca?" Cherry teased, out of earshot of Alan.

"Don't you dare," he snarled.

He had almost buried his anxiety concerning those missing papers. Why did she have to remind him?

CHAPTER 9

It was Saturday, the weekend, and Bridget picked up the letters from the mat and snuggled down on the settee with a cup of tea. Casually she flipped through the envelopes, discarding the obvious adverts and unwanted mail by tossing them on the floor, too lazy to aim for the bin from this distance. One of them hit the bottom shelf of the coffee table and knocked several old magazines off. They joined the other stuff on the floor, destined to stay there with them until she had eventually left the comfort of the deeply upholstered sofa.

Having poured herself a second cup, she returned to pick them up, tossing them on to the other cushion of the settee, next to which she plonked herself again. They were well out of date and she decided to flip through them, just in case there was something interesting design wise that she could cut out before she put them out for the dustbin.

She did not know why the Ryling Coffee advertisement particularly caught her attention this time. She had seen it plenty of times in the past. Sue, her business partner, had always drooled over the spreads featuring a group of handsome international rugby stars. You did not have to follow sport to appreciate these heart-throbs the moment they took their shirts off. They were hot property. The television advert had been an instant hit, becoming more popular than the 'Diet Coke 11.30 appointment' commercial. And one of them looked so like Matt. She smiled at the idea.

The advertisers had an exceptional commercial property, but they had taken that campaign off the TV and out of the magazines after one of the team had been seriously injured. Bridget suddenly shivered. Matt had said that he had been a rugby player and he had been injured. This had to be a coincidence surely. He was just any ordinary club rugby player, nothing more. Except she was beginning to have doubts, remembering Ray's interest and the boy's curious glances directed towards Matt. What if he was more famous than she thought?

She studied the photograph again, and found her gaze fixed on the features she knew so well; that familiar tantalizing grin, that slight stubborn flick of his fringe and those irresistible eyes that held you. Then she spotted it; a faint, tiny scar on his cheekbone, hardly distinguishable. It began to give her goose bumps. The whole idea was quite unnerving. No, no, it could not be, must not be him.

And yet it was. Despite the disguise of that rugged stubble and untidy hair, damn him, that was Matt in the photograph. He wasn't some casual amateur rugby player; he was a very famous one.

She sat trying to rationalize this. She did not want to admit it was him. It did not feel real.

She phoned her brother.

"Chris?"

Uh oh. It was the way she said it that warned him.

"I've been looking at that Ryling Coffee advert in the press."

"And?" he asked cautiously.

"It's Matt in the photo, isn't it?"

"Yes."

"It's not fair Chris, I thought he was just an ordinary injured sportsman. You should have told me."

"I tried to! But anyway, what difference does it make? You were the one who said it didn't matter what he had been before. That it wasn't important."

She was silent; Chris could hear her thinking.

"Is there anything else I should know?" she asked.

He was going to have to lie, again.

"I only searched the sport section after Ray tipped me off, to clarify his status," he said. "And to be honest, I don't see why it's a problem that he and his friends posed for some advert. Loads of people do it. It is not as if they are still in the limelight. He seems a decent sort of guy. I would still like to meet him," he added quickly, hoping to side-track her.

She ignored his hint and casually ended the call.

Now Chris felt worse. Hell! He had chickened out for a second time. He ought to have said more. Maybe now he would. But who was he kidding? It would be difficult. *Oh Ellen, why aren't you here to help me? I need you.*

Bridget had been calm. Of course, she had forgiven Matt for not being quite straight with her about who he was, and had understood why. He obviously did not want to upset her by admitting that he was a member of a team of handsome men who had been worshipped by most of the females in the country. But as she came to terms with this latest discovery and other fleeting remarks began to surface in her memory, and she found herself far from satisfied. Her friends used to mention the reports of their excessive partying from the celebrity magazines. The gossip did not please her, but she knew how to clarify her suspicions. The nearby reference library carried back numbers of newspapers and magazines. What else was she going to do, sit and ignore it?

The evidence was worse than she imagined. He and the rest of the team had partied with the beautiful and glamorous, dated striking models, and been seen in all the most exclusive places. Women adored them. Their about-town reputation was almost as legendary as their sporting prowess. The photos of their private lives had filled most of the glossy celebrity magazines. They were the envy of every other red-blooded male. Matt's public image was a shock.

"Oh Matt," she gulped.

She sat there on the sofa staring at his photo in the magazine. All her emotions were mixed up. It was too much to take in. Her eyes ached. How could she have been so dim, not to have realised his prevarication was a series of excuses to hide his past from her. She had taken everything he had told her at face value, because she wanted to believe what he said.

The fact that he was a sports personality she could put up with, but this celebrity life style showed a different side to him, one she did not like, one that changed her opinion of him. She was disappointed. She was hurt. Unfortunately, she had the rest of the day to brood on it, which was not a good thing. She paced, she sat, she paced, she sat. She was angry, she was calm.

Finally, she phoned Paula to tell her the news, her glum voice hardly hiding her heartache. Her sister meant to come up immediately to comfort her, but Bridget preferred to be alone. She would deal with it in her own way by having the rest of the day to herself, not that she was going to do anything except feel sorry for herself. She could not even think properly.

No sooner had Paula finished talking to her sister than she was heading for her husband, her face like thunder.

"You knew who he was, Ray. Poor Bridget! How could you keep that to yourself?"

Her words could be heard all over the house. The boys headed for their rooms to keep out of the way. This was clearly no place for them at the moment. They did not understand what was happening, except that their poor father was in deep trouble. They closed their door and lay on their beds, pulling faces at each other. This was such bad timing; they had been about to ask for tickets to the rugby match.

"I'm sorry sweetheart, but it's for them to sort this out," Ray told her very firmly.

"You thoughtless bastard!" Paula hit him, very, very hard. She was not going to forgive him for a long time.

"Get round here, NOW!" shouted Bridget down the phone.

Chris was only half awake. "It's Sunday morning. I was lying in. I haven't had breakfast yet." He yawned.

"Sod your breakfast! I want to see you!" Bridget yelled.

"Whatever it is, can't you tell me over the phone?"

She slammed down the phone so hard it made his ears ring. Then she hung up and went back to looking at the other back issues she had collected yesterday from the library. How could Matt do this to her? She was so angry.

Chris could tell this was serious, and he was at her house as soon as possible. He could see her eyes were slightly puffy from crying. She threw one of the magazines at him the instant he walked through the door, although by then he had worked out the cause of the drama. She had indeed found out more about Matt. Then he saw the magazine lying on the floor, open at the full-page spread showing Matt, with an iconic half grin, amid his friends, enjoying the company of a bunch of very glamorous models in a club.

Chris sat down, ready for a grilling.

"You RAT! Why didn't you tell me about this? How could you not tell me?"

"How could I Bridget? I did not want to cause a rift between you two," he argued.

"His photo was in all the papers. That was Matt!"

"Bridget, please do not get upset."

Not get upset! Was Chris that much of an idiot?

"Is there anything else you have deliberately forgotten?" she challenged him.

He shook his head, not as an answer, but as an indication of his frustration. How had he got caught in the middle of this?

"What am I supposed to do?" she went on. "I never imagined he was *that* well known. All those adverts, partying with a bunch of tarts, constantly splashed across the major celebrity magazines. All that public adoration!"

"Bridget, Bridget! He is not the same person. There is no indication that he hankers after that old lifestyle. From what I can gather, all that celebrity stuff is long over. Be honest, hasn't he proved that?"

"I can't believe you're defending him."

"I'm not. Just don't be too hasty in condemning him.

Don't give up on him, Bridget. Matt has been through a lot. He has lost a lot, but I believe he wants the stability you give him. He wants a new start. He wants you."

At the last remark, Bridget burst into tears. She wanted to believe Chris, but her mind was overwhelmed. The discovery of who Matt really was had come hard. It would take a great deal of getting used to. She was not sure she wanted to try.

"All that female attention. He had it all," Bridget mumbled.

She looked worn out, but Chris was going to do his best. He coughed nervously. How was he going to handle this? The last thing he was going to do was to add to her anguish by admitting that the posh sales brochure he had given to her and Paula some time ago, the one they had both drooled over so much, had showcased Matt's own flat in Richmond. He knew there was no point in denying the rest of Matt's history; the press photos had made sure that was impossible. His life had been too public. He had been too handsome, too charming, too everything. His track record was far from perfect. He was sure Matt really loved Bridget, but it was up to Matt to use all his charm to convince her how much.

"Bridget, that advertising campaign was simply publicity, to use their popularity, to make money for the sponsors. It promoted an image people liked. And as for all the media gossip about them, that was just to sell magazines. You shouldn't believe everything you read. I expect most of what they wrote about them is untrue or exaggerated."

Chris could see Bridget's mind was working overtime; it just needed a push in the right direction. "Remember what you have together. What do you love most about him? Let me guess. His touch, his wonderful eyes, his kiss, the smouldering soft growl in his throat which gives you goose bumps?"

Bridget blushed, a deep, embarrassed blush. She could not look at him. Her brother had never talked so openly about such intimate and delicate matters before. It quite shocked her. She could not believe this.

Chris grinned. "We're all human Bridget. Even me. You forget I had the pleasure of loving Ellen. How could I ever feel the same about any other female? The pure enjoyment of sharing yourself with a fascinating woman is unforgettable. There is nothing like it. Plus having a soulmate to fight over the TV control, wardrobe space, the toothpaste and the duvet. It's fun. It's love."

He had actually made her smile. Her pent-up tension had eased. There was hope for her yet.

"Have you spoken to Paula?" he asked.

"Of course. I had to put her off coming up yesterday while I absorbed everything, but she'll be here tomorrow, to stay over for a couple of days."

Thank goodness for that, thought Chris. He knew he wasn't exactly the best person for all this emotional drama.

"We'll have a long girlie talk. I'm sorry. I know all I did was feel sorry for myself earlier and then take it out on you," she concluded.

Chris had played his part, and she thanked him for it. She was feeling a lot better as they sat in the kitchen.

"You have to trust him," was his last piece of advice.

Bridget gave her brother a hug. Here was a man who never burdened others with his own feelings. After all, he rarely talked about how much he missed Ellen, although she knew he did.

"Where is Ellen now?"

"I wish I knew."

There was no regret or sadness in his voice, only affection. He was just waiting for her to return. When would he see her again? As long as it took – obviously. Yes, the space in the bed beside him remained empty, but it would not be forever. It just seemed like it, at times.

"I'll always remember the sight of you both covered in mud, that time you rescued that puppy from the ditch."

The memory made him smile. There was a twinkle in his eye. Memories of Ellen always warmed his soul and helped him carry on. The ongoing sabbatical trip she was making to the remotest corners of the globe to research animal survival was typical of her caring nature.

After Paula had spent a couple of days with her, Bridget made a decision. She announced that she was going away for a while on her own, probably to stay with Aunt Mary. She did not want to see or talk to Matt until she had sorted herself out. Her absence would not interfere with the business, because she could manage work via the internet and emails to Sue, her business partner. She could stay away as long as she liked – as if anyone could stop her.

"You will NOT tell him where I am," she instructed her brother.

Chris widened his eyes at the mere idea. As if Matt was likely to come to him, of all people. That would be the day!

She would have left Chris immediately, except the celebrations for the Queens 90th birthday were on the news. Some things were too nice to miss. There were occasions when a sense of affection for their monarch made people feel good inside. Chris hoped this would influence her attitude towards Matt.

He was going to volunteer to drive his sister to Cambridge, because after dropping Bridget off, it would allow him the opportunity to quickly nip over to Aston Hall for an hour. This was the chance he wanted to have a confidential word with the grandfather about Captain Tapley, the former owner of the estate. He should have done it before, when he was writing about the trouble at the Mews site, which the same man owned. He had failed to get all the facts, failed to get the full background. He had been lazy. He was getting stale. He should put that right and update his file for the future.

Chris walked through the courtyard towards the rear of Aston Hall, eager to find George Watson. There he was, the same as ever. With the same friendly grin, the old man shook Chris's hand very firmly.

"I'm pleased to see you again," he said. "I never thanked you for bring Rosie back into my life. Her visits have made such a difference."

Chris grinned. There was no need to answer. He explained why he had come and told Mr Watson about the article he had written on the mews, which had been also owned by Captain Tapley. At the time he had not bothered to find any extra information on him, but since he was coming this way, he hoped Mr Watson could provide some insight into Captain Tapley's character. Not that he expected much.

The old man gave it a lot of thought, but did not have much to contribute. The owner had left the country many, many years ago. And even when he was living there, Mr Watson had hardly seen him. He couldn't even remember what he looked like. He was a secret, private type, and disliked strangers in the house. The only thing he could remember was that he used to have various flashy businessmen from London visit him regularly. Not that anyone knew their names. He had assumed they were connected to his fine art business.

Chris made a few notes; it had not been a complete waste of time. He thanked the gardener and strolled back through the gardens. Then suddenly, a girl flew around the corner and nearly knocked him down. It was Rosie, wearing a chunky sweater, dungarees and wellingtons and carrying a bucket and a fork. Her face was glowing in the chilly air.

"How lovely. I haven't seen you for ages," she said. She took off the grubby working gloves and almost literally dragged him back towards the kitchen garden where Mr Watson was still working away, turning the earth in one of the vegetable plots.

Putting her bucket and fork aside, she had Chris's full attention.

"Chris, I don't suppose you've heard, but I've decided I am going to study horticulture, plants and garden design. I'm starting agricultural college next term. I can't wait. Isn't that lovely? I didn't realise how much I enjoyed being outside in the fresh air and tending plants. I think it was always in me. I just needed to find that spark. I've found it here at Aston Hall."

She babbled on happily, so full of her news, explaining that having spent time here, getting her hands dirty and learning about the care and growing of plants, she had realised that she had a natural talent for gardening. No doubt it was inherited from her father, who had been a groundsman and a gardener here. She was sure she had made the right decision.

Of course she had. Chris had never seen her look so utterly content. Her face glowed with happiness. Chris looked at the old man; there was little doubt he had encouraged her decision, and why not? Indeed it was clear that the pair of them were even more closely bound together than before, by their shared interest in horticulture and their love of the land. It explained her joy at being here all the time.

Callum had got it wrong; her presence here was not solely to do with Jake's memory. In a way Chris was relieved.

Although he felt he needed to take another look at the tree, to get everything in perspective. He recalled seeing Rosie at the old tree, and how tenderly she had touched its ancient bark.

"Would you mind if I took a look at the tree?" he asked cautiously.

"The tree? Yes, if you want." She sighed.

"You don't want to come with me?"

She shook her head, although she did not seem put out at his suggestion or concerned by his curiosity. She followed him to the fence, where she sat happily swinging her legs and watched him as he made his way down to the bottom field.

Chris stood there, taking it all in. He glanced at the small wooden cross amongst the gnarled roots, placed there in Jake's memory. The tree was very old and the branches were brittle; it was clear it had been unsafe to climb for a long time, which made him wonder why Jake had tried to climb it. These were country children, they would know better. Especially Jake! It was no good, Chris was sure Jake would not have climbed the tree, despite the evidence of the broken branches around him. The inquest report of accidental death had not allowed for the very nature of the child to be taken into consideration. He looked at the stumps of lower old broken branches. They were not that high, he could touch them if he reached up. Could Jake really have died falling from there?

"That's a very big tree," he commented on his return.

She nodded, showing no emotion at all.

"Did anyone, er – see him fall?" he asked softly.

"No. Apparently not."

She jumped down beside him and they made their way back through the gardens.

"Let's go in and have a look around the main house," he said as they approached the front of the period building.

"No thank you," she declared, rather firmly.

"Oh, come on."

"It's just a dilapidated old building."

She gave a nervous laugh and started talking about the gardens again. Chris shrugged disappointedly and left her to walk to the front door, where he waited for a moment, hoping she would change her mind.

The inside of the house was empty and sad, and his footsteps echoed on the bare floorboards. It was indeed very dilapidated. No wonder she did not want to come inside. He remembered Callum showing him her drawing of the hallway and staircase. It was not an inspiring view, in Chris's opinion. In fact, there was nothing special about the whole house, to his mind.

He finished the tour and headed outside, to find Rosie waiting for him.

"See you again soon," she said with a smile as she waved him off.

Chris drove away, but stopped as soon as he came to a pub. He wanted to think this out, to make sense of the irrational suspicions which kept floating around in his brain. Why did Jake's death still niggle him? It was years ago. He felt the hairs on the back of his neck bristle. What if… If Jake had not fallen from the tree, then he must have fallen somewhere else. He needed to get back to Aston Hall. He finished his pint and got back into his car.

Back at the hall he walked back through the courtyard, part of him wondering why he was doing this. Fortunately, there was no sign of Rosie. George Watson was still working away turning the earth.

"I thought you were on your way back to London," he remarked.

"I was. I…"

Something made him pause. This wonderful old gardener was the salt of the earth, and so genuine. What was he going to say?

George put aside his spade and waited.

"Would you mind if I asked you about Jake?"

"Not at all. What is bothering you in particular?" George asked sympathetically.

"I hate to bring this up. I don't mean to be insensitive – I know it's a delicate matter, but for some insane reason – and I am sorry to say this - I don't believe Jake could have died falling out of that tree."

There – he had said it.

The old man took a sharp intake of breath, suddenly looking unsteady. Chris quickly took his arm to give support. He had not meant to cause distress.

"Forgive me, I did not mean to upset you."

"No, it's all right." There was a long pause before he continued. "I hadn't expected to find anyone who thought the same thing. We were all so devastated at his loss. In our grief nothing else mattered. We did not question the inquest findings. Why should we? It was a long time later I had my doubts, but I didn't want to face them. I didn't want to think it was anything except an accident. A simple accident, one that was easy to accept. How could it be anything else?"

"But every time I look at that oak tree, I wonder. There was no reason for Jake to climb that tree. It was unsafe. He had never done such a stupid thing before, so why would he?" He shook his head thoughtfully.

Chris's imagination was now in overdrive, focusing his mind on every detail. He had to think logically. There was no reason for Jake to climb that isolated tree. Therefore he hadn't. If he had fallen down somewhere else and been concussed, he would hardly have stumbled all the way down to the tree before dying. And if he had found his way there, how did the broken branches fit in? Had someone found him and maybe moved him? Why would they do that?

"So, what else are you *not* saying?" the old man asked quietly.

"That I don't think he climbed the tree at all. He might have fallen down somewhere else."

"I had considered that, but where could have fallen, and why go down to the tree? It doesn't make sense does it?"

No, it did not. Chris did not have an answer. If it had

been an ordinary accident, there would be no need to move him. Unless wherever he fell would be inconvenient for someone and would have had people asking questions.

His mind kept going back to Rosie's drawing of the hallway and her continual reluctance to go into the building. Did it mean anything? Had something happened in the house? If Jake had fallen down inside the house, he would have been found there. There would be no need to move him.

"I don't have a clue. I should not have mentioned it really. I am sorry."

The old man sighed. "It would have been nice to find an explanation after all these years. Never mind, it doesn't alter my affection for him."

"I do have another question, if you don't mind. Nothing to do with Jake. The last thing Rosie had drawn in her precious sketch book was the interior of the house. I wondered if there was any special reason for it?"

The old man smiled and nodded. "Ah, that's easy to explain. It was the last time they were together. They were caught out by a thunderstorm and sheltered in the porch. Then they crept inside and hid under the stairs to avoid the owner. Rosie started to draw as they waited for the rain to stop. Jake died the next day. After that, everything changed."

There was a silence while Chris took it all in and considered it. Yes, it made sense.

"What are you thinking?" Mr Watson looked enquiringly at Chris.

Chris found himself smiling. "I'm thinking that Rosie is happy here. She looks so at peace with the world, so radiant. You both love this place. I shouldn't have bothered you."

And he meant it. If Rosie had come to terms with whatever had happened here, why should he ruin that with his damn curiosity? And that was all it was – his curiosity. He was willing to leave it alone. He shrugged off and walked back along the terrace to the car. The drive home would be tiresome and boring.

A week or two went by without any word from Bridget; not that he really expected to hear from her until she wanted to come home. After he had been food shopping, Chris had just put the last of the tins in the cupboards when there was a knock on the front door. He opened to it to find someone he had never expected to see. It was Matt Hillier. This was the first time he had seen him in the flesh.

"Good God! I never expected you to come here. Are you sure you aren't lost?" Chris could not help being slightly sarcastic. "You do know this is the enemy camp, the home of one of the dreaded newshounds."

"I wouldn't have come unless I had to!" came Matt's terse reply.

"Obviously." Chris shrugged.

Matt did not flinch; he didn't mind being barracked. It did not mean much after the recent days of uncertainty. Matt had not yet been aware of Bridget's latest decision to disappear, or had declared a cooling-off period between them. It had taken a while longer for him to realise that the lack of contact with Bridget was dragging on too long. He had already suffered, having camped outside Bridget's home in the car for hours and knocked on neighbour's doors without being able to trace where she had gone. She was not a missing person, so he couldn't ask the police. Why had she just walked away? He was beginning to question his whole purpose in this.

Matt nodded. "I admit I wasn't sure… whether to come or not."

"Well now you have. You had better come in. I'm not going to bite," Chris joked.

He showed Matt into the lounge and bade him sit. Matt looked tired and uncomfortable, but he had come for a reason, and Chris could wait.

"I don't know why you're hesitating," said Chris. "Come on, get it said."

"Do you know where Bridget is?"

"I'm not allowed to tell you," Chris answered calmly.

"I expected you to say that. I have already been in touch with her sister and her business partner, with the same result."

They had all given him the same reply. They all knew, and they had all been stubbornly unhelpful. Without being unpleasant to him, they had all closed ranks. So why did he think Chris would be any different, this press man who must know all about his colourful past? He of all people would be less than sympathetic to his cause; he could turn out to be his toughest adversary. Had he expected Chris to tell him where Bridget was? Highly unlikely. He could not exactly force it from him.

Chris was also thinking, as he took in every inch of the powerful athlete Matt had once again become. He had realised he would be the last one on the list for Matt to contact. Now here he was, prepared to confront his nemesis.

"I don't understand," said Matt. "I hadn't realised she was deliberately staying away from me. I thought it was just pressure of work."

Maybe he really did not know. Who would have told him? His ignorance was clear, so Chris decided to put his out of his misery.

"Matt, I think you're in trouble. She saw your old Ryling Coffee ad in a magazine, and pictures of you and the team out on the town."

Matt stared at him, his eyes wide in disbelief. He shook his head.

"Hell! No way! She doesn't follow the society sheets or the celebrity circus. How could that happen?"

"But it has. This is the real world we live in. You can't pretend that your celebrity status didn't exist."

"I didn't want to hurt her. What do I do?" He sounded defeated.

"Why ask me? She's struggling to accept what you were. She doesn't want to talk to you at the moment. It won't be easy, so don't think otherwise."

There was no animosity as Chris offered Matt his advice

and a drink. Matt looked like he could do with one. The guy was stumped and floundering in a quagmire of regret.

"When is she coming back?"

"Again, honestly I have no idea."

"I didn't mean to mess up. I adore your sister. She's funny, feisty – wonderful to be with..."

"Stubborn, wilful, determined," Chris interrupted kindly, leaning forward to top up his glass.

"Encouraging and supportive," Matt finished, smiling.

"Then don't give up. I want Bridget to be happy."

Chris liked this guy. All he saw was a man who really cared about his sister. He smiled to himself, secretly hoping Bridget wouldn't be too hard on him. Matt's stance, build, direct gaze and firm set of the jaw indicated he was strong enough to deal with the rest of the world these days, and more than capable of putting any nosy newshound in his place. But dealing with Bridget was another matter. He could only hope it would work out. It was out of his hands.

Matt had been annoyed that no one had told him the reason for Bridget's absence, except, of all people, her brother. Chris had surprised him. He was nothing like Matt had expected; he had been perfectly calm and reasonable. He had not taken sides or not been angry about the circumstances for this latest setback. He had attributed no blame and uttered no critical remarks. He had even joked about being one of the dreaded journalists and about Bridget's characteristics.

He had underestimated this brother; Chris seemed a decent and fair man. He was glad he had met him.

Matt returned home and wandered around the farm, soaking up the peace and quiet. He sat on the old tractor, cursing his luck, but philosophically accepting that he had got it wrong. So much for the excuse he had made to himself for his secretive attitude. Why had he gambled on the forlorn hope of keeping his past from Bridget and kept putting off divulging anything? It no longer seemed necessary. They were happy as they were, to such a point that he was sure it would not matter much when she did find out. But it had. She had walked away without talking to him.

Had he been selfish, expecting her to dismiss it so easily? He had thought their attachment was solid enough to survive. He should not have been that stupid. But he could not change the past; he was what he was. He could only hope she would understand that; that he had become the man she wanted. He had stopped letting the uncertainty put a dampener on his life these days. Gone were those periods of self-doubt. He had to get his new career organised. He was going to be busy, and he had been improving other aspects of his life. He had been in touch with his former team mates. Common sense had kicked in at last. He had had to do something to repair the damage between them. It was either going to work or not, he told himself. It had worked. He found himself swamped by their genuine enthusiasm and delighted to see him again and find out how he was. Their first meeting was nothing like as awkward as it could have been. He guessed that was mainly due to his brother Mike, who had kept in touch with them regularly. He had a lot to thank his older, wiser brother for.

Matt had since been out for a beer with them to talk over old times. They were glad to have him back in their company. The old camaraderie was slowly being restored. They had remained his loyal friends, and had not given up on him despite his continual selfish determination to shut them out and ignore them. They had understood his reasons; they had changed too, after the trauma of that night. They were still bound together despite never speaking of it. They had protected him at the hospital. They had kept the important aspects of the incident from the public. Their statements were in a closed police file.

He admitted he had been stubborn, moody, awkward and cantankerous. To which they heartily agreed, as if they would let to let him off that easily, now he was back in the fold. "Nothing new there then," one of them joked.

Life was looking good, he had told them. He had plans. He was in the process of sorting out his finances and arranging various training courses. He had no regrets, but he had expected Bridget to be part of his future.

CHAPTER 10

The following Friday, Bridget phoned Chris to say she wanted to come home. Being away had not really solved anything, she told him. He gave a reassuring reply and promised he would be up there the next day.

He quickly wrapped up his work and tidied his desk. There was nothing urgent to cover. He also took the chance to have a sneaky look through the sheet of photos taken at the Marriott event which had been left on Cherry's desk. He spotted Francesca in several of the shots, but luckily there were none of the Italian Casanova lurking in the background. He was pleased at this suggestion that their association had ended. She deserved to prosper without the undesirable influence of his presence in her life. He could not help being judgmental.

Before he drove north to collect Bridget from Cambridge, he phoned ahead to ask Aunt Mary where Rosie would be. His aunt laughed, for where else would she be but at Aston Hall, gardening with Jake's grandfather. Perfect! Another detour on his journey was on the cards. The previous night, for some unknown reason, his nagging curiosity about Jake and Rosie had resurfaced and his mind had returned to the events at Aston Hall. He could not let it go. He hoped he could satisfy his curiosity.

It was May and the gardens were a showcase of colour. No wonder Rosie loved being here, but where-abouts was she? In frustration he scanned the grounds from the terrace, his lips pursed, his frown deepening, until eventually he spotted her in jovial conversation with Jake's grandfather. They were happily strolling slowly through the gardens, looking at plants. When she saw Chris hurrying to join them, Rosie skipped across the lawn to meet him.

"Hello Chris. What a lovely day. It's great for working outdoors. You should try it."

He smiled at her remarks and then led her slightly away from the house, knowing that bright that charming expression would change if he continued. He was about to be responsible for that, but there was no going back. He was here for a purpose. How was he to begin? Anywhere would do.

"Callum mentioned that the last drawing in your book was of inside the house."

"Yes," she sighed. "It was the last place I had been with Jake. I never wanted to draw anything after that."

Her words were so wistful and philosophical. She had nothing to hide. She had spoken readily about it without any sign of faltering or having to choose her words carefully, and it was such a simple, plausible explanation. No wonder she wouldn't go into the main house. It must hurt her to see the last place they had shared, without him there. It made so much sense. And it confirmed what he already knew; the reason for the last picture being drawn and why she didn't go back inside the house. Both were perfectly understandable.

Chris looked around before continuing. George Watson was tending a patch in the flower beds, out of earshot.

"I thought you weren't allowed in the house?" Chris asked innocently.

"It was only the once. It was the nearest place to shelter out of the rain."

"The day after your drawing, did you go back inside?"

"What? Of course not. Why would I?" She looked surprised.

Had he got it all wrong? He frowned. Was he making too much of this? Rosie was Rosie. Rosie had never lied because she had never had to, but Chris felt these circumstances might be different. The case was still up for debate. He would have to continue.

"I want to understand what happened that day."

"Why? What has got into you? Why do you want to drag it all up after all this time? What does it matter to you what happened? It's nothing to do with you!" she snapped between gritted teeth, trying not to raise her voice. Her eyes were narrowed, then wide and flaring, her shoulders tense. "Jake died. It was an accident!"

"Without witnesses?"

"Stop this! What the hell is wrong with you?"

Suddenly Chris felt a firm hand on his shoulder. It was George.

"What on earth is going on here?" The old gardener stepped in to confront Chris.

"It's all right, Gramps. There's nothing to worry about. I won't be bullied."

She snatched herself free, turned her back and marched off, then stopped by the archway to turn and glare at Chris. He took a deep breath to compose himself. He was far from satisfied, but he felt a little space might be advisable at the moment.

"Is this about Jake again?" asked George.

Chris nodded.

"Is something troubling you?"

"I still don't believe he died anywhere near that damn tree, and I don't think you do either. I suddenly thought Jake might have been in the house for some reason that morning, although I can't think why. And if Jake had fallen inside, why would he have been found by the tree? Even concussed I can't imagine he would have managed to wander down there, or wanted to."

"So, there's nothing to suggest he was inside?"

"No."

Chris pressed his tongue into his cheek to stop himself from adding, 'unless someone moved him.'

Rosie, who had been watching the men as they talked, rushed back to the gardener's side.

"What's wrong? What has he been saying?" she demanded.

At which the old man took her hand, patted it and told her not to fuss. "There's something I want you to tell me," he said. "However difficult. Rosie, was there any reason Jake would have gone back into the house that morning?"

A bewildered Rosie looked into his gentle, understanding features. Chris waited, knowing her answer would clarify his suspicions or dispel them.

"Not that I can think of. Well… I'm not sure. I had left some pencils behind. We were going to retrieve them when the owner was out. But obviously we never did. I forgot all about them. I never gave them another thought."

There was silence as George looked meaningfully at Chris. "You think Jake might have gone back for the pencils, and something happened there?"

"It does seem probable."

The old man frowned. "But he had no pencils with him when he was found. Which suggests he might not have been in the house."

"Were the pencils ever found? Anywhere?" Chris asked. It was another part of the puzzle; it could be a clue as to where Jake had really had his accident.

George shook his head. Since no one knew Rosie had left them in the house, no one would have ever looked for them there.

Rosie, who had been listening intently, was stunned by what was being said. She suddenly shuddered, looking at one to the other, her eyes wide. She began to tremble as she began to realise what might have happened. Her lip quivered and tears appeared.

"You think he went back inside because of me, to look for my pencils. Then whatever happened is all my fault. I'm responsible," she said.

"No, no Rosie, we are just speculating," said George. "That's what silly men do. Indeed, why should we assume he was in the house? There's no proof he was." He drew her into his chest, trying to soothe her.

Chris stood there frozen to the spot, staring at her reaction. He had never expected her to blame herself. His jaw dropped. Christ, what had he done? What a terrible notion to inflict on her. How could he have been so completely stupid, stupid, *stupid?*

The old man continued to rock Rosie in his arms with her head nestled into his shoulder until the tears gradually stopped. She took his hankie to wipe her face and sat holding his hand, now calm and quiet. Chris was trying to think how to make amends, how to undo the damage he had caused.

"Honestly, I didn't mean any of it, Rosie. I was just rambling. You know what I'm like. My imagination runs riot. Forgive me," he pleaded.

"How could you think like that? I hate you!"

"I'm sorry. Please Rosie, you should not take any notice of me. I..."

Then George spoke. "That's enough. All this theorising is a waste of time. It happened years ago. Jake has gone. We can't bring him back. Why do we have to torment ourselves?"

He hugged Rosie and kissed the top of her head, then looked up at Chris again. "Do you think Rosie would be so happy here if Jake's death had caused her any concern? Of course not! All this worthless conjecture has only created more questions than answers. Jake could have been anywhere. We don't know, we will never know. We don't need to know. Do we, Mr Page?"

Chris shook his head, wanting to agree. All he had was supposition. Chris could see that George was abandoning his own doubts about the accident to protect Rosie. He could not argue with him in front of her, it would not be fair. He was the villain here, no one else.

"I'm sorry. I didn't mean..."

Rosie stepped up to him and looked him in the eye. Chris knew she would not forgive him.

"I hate you, Chris Page. How dare you do this! It was cruel. The truth, whatever may or may not have happened, can't change anything. Jake died. All we have is a cherished memory. And I won't let you destroy or undermine my memories of him. I won't have it!"

Chris knew he should leave. He was still convinced that he was on the right track about Jake's death, but after today he could hardly pursue it further. If there was a secret, it would never be unearthed.

He plodded back to the car, scuffing the ground as he went. This had been an utter disaster. Sod it!

Yet he could not stop thinking about it all. Was there really any significance, any connection with that hallway, even one Rosie did not know about? He could not help wondering if she herself had gone back inside the next day. He didn't want to believe such a possibility, that she might have seen something, but what if she had? She would surely not have kept it secret. He frowned. Every logic told him, he had to leave it alone. It was not easy.

Chris arrived at Aunt Mary's home to find Bridget packed and waiting for him.

"Did you call in to see Rosie on your way?" she asked.

"Yes."

Bridget gave him a curious look.

"Was she OK?"

"We... we didn't part on the best of terms."

He sighed heavily, and she raised her eyebrows. "Wow! So what happened?"

"I'll tell you later. Come on, are you ready to leave?"

No sooner were they in the car and driving off than Bridget was demanding to know what had gone on. It was difficult to explain while driving, but she kept badgering him, so he pulled into a layby. There he relayed the gist of the matter to Bridget, including his doubts and suspicions about Jake. She was not impressed.

"You utter numskull! How could you! Being curious and caring is fine, but Rosie is family, you should have kept your theories to yourself. I doubt she will talk to you again. And as for Aunt Mary, heavens, I can only imagine the ear-bashing you're in for when she hears of your behaviour. You'll have to phone her when we get home and apologise."

Duly put in his place, Chris started the car again and they continued their journey in silence, making for a strange atmosphere. He glanced at his sister. She still hadn't mentioned anything about Matt or what she was going to do.

"So, are you going to see Matt?" he asked.

"Oh yes," she told him quite firmly. "I have to. I can't go on like this. In hindsight I shouldn't have run away. I should have had it out with him there and then. I wasn't thinking straight."

"That sounds ominous."

"The thought of Matt being different from the man I thought I knew is hard. I did not like the idea that he was more famous off the field than on it. What does he expect me to do?"

"Just don't be too hasty to condemn him. No one's perfect. Don't be too hard on him. A little tact and kindness would help resolve the situation."

"That's a bit rich coming from you. You didn't show any tact in your fracas with Rosie today, did you?"

Chris said nothing. He could hardly feel more guilty than he already did.

"I don't intend to be part of that crazy life of his once he's back in circulation," she said.

"Bridget, when has he ever indicated that he would go back to his old lifestyle? He doesn't intend to be back in circulation, as you put it."

She huffed; she was not so sure. She had seen a paragraph in a newspaper which reported that Matt had been seen out having a drink with some of his former team mates.

"Yes, I believe he has been mending bridges with his old friends, but nothing more," said Chris. "That was what you wanted. You were the one who insisted he had to be more sociable, so you can't complain when he is. He came to my place looking for you, desperate to find you. He cares. There's no way he will give up on you."

"No? But things are different."

Chris knew Matt would try to put it right. He might regret the past, but he couldn't change it. He had to live with it. Everyone made mistakes. Hadn't he just proved that?

"No one can turn back the clock. You're both sensible enough to get through this," were Chris's final remarks on the subject as he took her bags in through the front door.

"You're getting very philosophical in your old age."

"Old age? What a cheek!"

"Just go and make that call to Aunt Mary."

Chris headed for the phone, ready to eat humble pie, but his aunt gave him little chance to speak. She already knew about his confrontation with Rosie and he was very definitely in the doghouse. Her voice was angry, sharp and unforgiving. She was furious with him and told him he was banned from visiting for the foreseeable future.

Chris gulped. He had not expected such a severe barrage from his normally mild-mannered aunt.

"Once Callum hears about this, you'll have more trouble on your hands," she said finally. Then she hung up.

"Serves you right," Bridget told him. "When will you learn to control this curious obsession of yours? Your imagination has really got you into trouble this time."

Chris returned home feeling absolutely wrecked. He had been so stupid. He had handled his enquiry into Jake's death with the same blunt intensity he used in his work. He should have been able to separate the two. He was feeling really down. He had lost track of who he was recently. What had come over him? All this self-analysis was not helping his self-esteem. He had always thrived on the hustle and bustle of his job, but he was not enjoying that as much as he used to. He was still ashamed of his mistake with Francesca, and now he had added another to the list.

Not long afterwards he had a phone call from Callum, who was very laid back about the whole Rosie incident and told him how he had chuckled when his mother had told him about his altercation with Rosie. He was laughing, genuinely laughing.

"I believe 'never darken my doorstep again' is mother's quote of the week. Poor you," he joked.

Far from the expected rollicking from Callum, all he got was sympathy.

"Thanks Chris," he joked.

"You're not angry?"

"Why should I be? We were both curious about Rosie's last drawing. You were the one brave enough to ask her. I should thank you. At least it put me back in her good books," he continued cheerfully.

Chris went on to tell him everything she had said. He could remember every word.

"Crikey! So, there's no mystery about the drawing of the hallway after all?"

"It seems that way."

"You don't seem satisfied."

"I still think Jake went back for the missing pencils, but it's an unprovable theory, one I have to keep to myself. I've caused enough trouble."

The conversation drifted into Callum's recent neglect of his studies. Using the excuse of a birthday, he and his friends had succumbed to the effects of an extreme night of drinking. They had celebrated too much. He went on to relay the harsh reality of a sore head and tidying a wrecked flat, as if no one else had ever suffered either. Chris let him chatter on, whilst putting in the odd word to pretend interest for the sake of being polite. He raised his eyebrows and yawned; he had almost forgotten his own youthful exploits. They seemed so long ago, but no doubt they had been just the same. Nothing really changed.

Bridget and Matt arranged to meet in the garden of the rural riverside pub they had been to before. It was a quiet spot where their privacy would not be interrupted.

When Bridget arrived Matt was already sitting there on a bench. He had his eyes closed, locked away in his own thoughts. They were two people who belonged together. Or did they? He had worked hard to get this far, but what if Bridget wasn't interested in how much he had achieved? Hell, if she had not run away so quickly, he would have had the opportunity to tell her all his latest plans.

He opened his eyes as she sat down beside him, and thought she looked prettier than ever. He took her hand, gently wrapping his fingers in hers, because he didn't know what else to do. Just to hold her hand felt comforting. He was not sure what to say to her or what to expect.

He could tell that she was not sure what she was going to say to him either. He felt their meeting might be emotional and fragile. He could not read her at all; she didn't seem angry, she did not smile or avoid his eyes.

Her first words startled him.

"We can't go on like this. This is never going to work."

She sounded... he wasn't sure what.

"Why? Nothing has changed between us. I am still the same person you met at the garden centre."

"No, you're not. Your sporting reputation, that coffee advert and the way you used to live can't be ignored. What you were does make a difference. Why didn't you tell me?"

"Because I was worried you wouldn't like me. Would you

have listened? Would you have understood? I didn't want to destroy what we had."

There was no point in pretending or denying his past behaviour, the press photos had made sure of that. His life had been too public. He didn't blame her for criticising him. How could he apologise for being him?

"We have seen better days."

"Oh Bridget, please. I can't alter the past. I admit I enjoyed myself. I succumbed to flirtations, assignations, call them what you like. I admit my track record is far from perfect, but – that's in the past. I don't move in those circles any more and neither do the rest of the team. We have moved on. We are different people – better people."

"Matt, I am not going to punish myself with false hope. This is not going to work. We don't stand a chance."

"What do you mean?"

"You still have the quality to turn heads. You'll be the target for every stunning beauty."

Matt was thunderstruck. How could she imagine he was that fickle? After all they had been through together, the difficult, the good and bad. He had to reassure her. He had to find the right words, except he was not good with finding the right words off the cuff. Why was this so hard?

"But I don't want anyone else. I wouldn't let anyone drive us apart. Why would I?" he whispered softly.

"Oh Matt. What is the point? What are we doing to each other?"

"How can you say that!"

"You! You are... you're too famous," she sighed, almost afraid to say it.

"I'm not famous anymore!" he declared, dismissing the idea. He took her in his arms, held her softly against him. She nestled into his shoulder. "Stop this, please. Listen, I have made some important decisions about my future. I need you to be part of them," he murmured.

She did not want to discuss it any more, but it was too easy to lean into this battered, torn and weary but wonderful example of manhood. The sensitive touch of his fingers moved down her cheek to tilt her chin. Hell, this man did not need words, he knew what he was doing. Bridget blushed. Her heart was beating so fast she was sure he could hear it. She had lost the battle. Heavens, what sort of man was this?

"Are we still good?" he asked, his eyes firmly fixed on hers.

Bridget nodded, smiled and gently squeezed his hand. Of course, they were. She would gladly take one day at a time for as long as it lasted. Whether it was for a week, a month, a year or longer, she did not care. She would treasure every second with him and enjoy it without regret, without thinking about the past, the doubts or the what ifs. She did not want any promises he couldn't keep. She loved him unconditionally.

"All I want is a normal life, to share my days with you," Matt declared with as much conviction as he could muster. They had run out of things to say for the moment. Instead they were content to make their way casually back across the gardens, still holding hands. All the old familiarity of the past had returned as if by magic.

"I called in on your brother while you were away," he confided.

"He told me."

The family were truly delighted that the rift was healed. Everyone relaxed. Life settled back to normal, with Matt more determined than ever to prove his commitment to Bridget. He did not mind crowds, they went out more, he took her to the cinema. He was getting on fine with Paula and Ray's family, often accompanying Bridget when she visited them. He seemed to take being in their company in his stride. Even the boys were over their stage of just staring silently in awe at him. Now they had so many questions; like Ray, they wanted the inside stories about the games, the places they had played and the other players. Failing that, simply to talk about sport in general, including football. Not that Matt followed football, although he knew enough to appreciate Leicester City winning the Premier League recently. He always supported the underdog.

Matt might not play rugby any more, but he managed to cause great excitement when he offered the boys his complimentary tickets for some of the games, a gesture which had him buried by arms and legs as the boys threw themselves bodily at him. Ray was also delighted and kept expressing his thanks. Bridget and Paula watched, taking it all in.

Matt's association with Chris was a little different, since they did not see each other that often, although Matt was gradually getting used to the brief, casual exchanges with him.

The next time Matt called in to pick up Bridget from Chris's place, Chris could not help noticing that it was obvious Matt still worked out at the gym.

"She won't be long. She's just popped up to the corner shop," Chris told him. As Matt settled down to wait, Chris could not help some light-hearted teasing.

"No plans for a remake of the coffee advert? I'm surprised you haven't been approached for another Ryling campaign."

"Actually, we have. The team's reunion sparked off a lot of new interest. The rest of the team are considering it. They want me to join them, but I won't."

"And that's not simply because Bridget prefers to keep your body to herself?" Chris said with a grin.

"Christ! That's a bit personal."

"But true." Chris laughed. "There's no need to be shy about it."

He hoped he had done enough to prove he intended to treat Matt in exactly the same way as his sister, with honesty and a good dose of humour. He poured Matt a drink and they continued to chat on quite amicably, Chris keeping the conversation centred on their expectations.

"Now we have to put things straight between us. I wanted us to have a home together," Matt confessed, quite openly.

"Wow, that's a big step. Do you know what you're in for?"

"We'll muddle through."

"Muddle being the operative word here. You do realise she has a tendency to be – untidy? There are knick-knacks of hers buried all over the house."

"How so? Her place always looks spick and span."

"She does have a habit of bringing her work home. You'll have to allow space for the artwork and other rubbish Bridget will want to offload into a new place. I suggest you'll need extra storage room or even a spare outbuilding. The words 'chaos' and 'clutter' come to mind," Chris added mischievously.

Matt gave a deep sigh. Did he care? Heck no. Having her stuff all about the house appealed to him.

"Well, with most of my stuff gone, there are plenty of empty boxes she can have. She could take her stuff to the tip or a Sunday car boot sale. Or is that being too optimistic, Chris? Do you think she will throw much away?"

"Doubtful." They both grinned.

"Would you tell me one more thing?" Chris yawned lazily.

Matt frowned at his host, wondering what was coming.

"Am I right in thinking that you were the client who paid to have Le Bistro almost empty when you took her there?" Chris knew he must have money from the fees for the advertising, so it was a pretty secure bet that he was right. Matt had hardly been strapped for cash, despite what they had thought.

Matt's smile answered the question. He had not minded the exorbitant fee to ensure their privacy for that exclusive meal with her.

"It was worth it," he said.

This light-hearted banter between them was refreshing, and Chris's casual approach to making Matt's acquaintance was going well. They laughed together, which was a good sign. Then, out of the blue, Matt suggested that he should come out for a drink some time with him and his brother. Chris could see he meant it, and Chris was certainly not going to turn the chance down.

Soon enough, true to Matt's word, Chris found himself meeting Matt's brother shortly after. For a policeman he seemed an ordinary bloke, and he made no reference to the problems he must deal with on a day-to-day basis. Mike shook his hand and smiled; he was here to make friends, nothing more.

Which he did, as the brothers soon enthralled Chris with their tales of growing up on a farm. There were the hay fights in the barn, chasing the chickens, climbing the tall cherry ladders and making forts out of packing boxes. Their youthful experiences had him laughing out loud. Nothing was false or put on. This was who they were.

Chris tried to match their stories by relating the problems he had had, having two sisters and being outnumbered at every turn. Forced to play tennis with them and go to dance lessons, he preferred books, music and old movies. The three of them were open about admitting their own foibles. It was good to find common ground between them. The easy banter and chit-chat, laced with a few quirky jokes, was a sure sign their 'getting to know you' evening had been a success.

Chris was now in the mood for doing something constructive with his spare time, and that did not include painting the bathroom. He headed off to help Mal build that new garden shed. He didn't mind banging in a few nails, sawing wood and getting splitters, as long as Mal was sure they were following the instructions. They had a few mishaps, but eventually they finished and were able to sit back and admire their handiwork. Finally they tightened up all the screws and gave the shed a good shake to test its stability.

"Well, I can't believe we did that," said Mal.

"Just don't advertise us as handymen, at least not yet," Chris joked.

Mal took him for a drink at the local as a reward, and brought him up to date with Mrs Cooper's enterprise. The Old Toy Shop had been turned into a book shop, and it was thriving. "Come on," he said, "get your coat, we can pop round now. You'll be surprised at the transformation."

Chris wasn't sure what to expect, having seen Nathan's photos of the original tired building. When he saw it, it gladdened his heart. It had been improved beyond recognition. The front of the shop was freshly painted and styled as a period Victorian book store, with bowed windows either side of a central door. It was a step back in time, oozing a wonderful comforting charm. Chris's eyes lit up. He was delighted to see the shelves bursting with books of all kinds. He could not help himself running his hands along the rows and picking up one book after another. The customers were similarly enthralled, browsing around the interior and often stopping at the large display by the counter, where she had incorporated the posters of the antique toys. They took pride of place and were set out sympathetically to show off their exquisite individual designs.

Now and again the loud brass bell over the front door would clang as people entered or left, and Mrs Cooper would smile to herself. She looked content, and Chris felt pleased for her. Her hard work had turned this into a treasure. According to Mal, she wanted to have a children's corner where they could sit, read and talk to her about the stories. It sounded enchanting. She deserved her success, although Chris could see she would need an extra hand to run the shop if it continued to be so busy. If only he was free, if only he did not have a full-time job, he could easily have settled for working here. Here he could switch off from the world and bury himself in pleasant dreams.

Then, out of nowhere, Chris received a letter from Rosie, saying she had forgiven him for his insane curiosity. Everyone had wanted answers, but there were none, and she hoped he could accept that, she wrote. The letter went on in her usual scribbled hand to tell him about a metal pencil case she had buried at the tree. She wrote: 'Inside is a note for him in my best handwriting, a small piece of folded paper, thanking him for being my friend. It is there for prosperity.'

He read the letter twice before folding it and put it away, thinking it seemed a fitting end to all his curiosity. Except it wasn't; he knew it would be hard to forget. He hated it when there were matters that would never have answers. What had happened to the missing pencils? No one had mentioned them. Were they left in the house and discarded by the owner? Stop this, he told himself. He was going round in circles. Again.

CHAPTER 11

Matt had tagged along with the rest of the team for their first photo shoot for the new Ryling Coffee campaign. He stayed in the background watching all the sets for the still photos. They were to show several of the team settled at different café sites around the city, obviously drinking coffee. This time they had changed the whole concept for the videos; it would start with some of them in the gym, some of them in the park, walking through the markets and touring the landmarks of London. Each of the small groups ending up at a coffee shop somewhere in the capital, at which point a multi-screen would picture them all at the same time, with the caption 'There's always time for a Ryling coffee'. The plan was to expand, using different famous cities, as the campaign grew.

Matt left them to it, as he had seen enough. He did not miss being part of that activity, or any part of the publicity. The team were still enjoying themselves, posing in a flippant, uncooperative manner and teasing each other, to the frustration of the photographer. There were many close-ups showing their smiling faces and their mischievous eyes to tempt the female audience, but nothing more extreme. Matt smirked to himself; there were many females who were going to be disappointed now that the familiar show of bare flesh had been ditched.

No one had bothered him at the studio, recognised him or asked his name. The social media were hardly interested in him these days. His reunion with his team mates proved that. An earlier paragraph in the mainstream papers had barely raised an eyebrow. He was pleased he was not newsworthy anymore, and nor did he miss playing rugby. He would have had to have given it up at some time; it had just happened a lot earlier than he had expected. He had convinced himself that it was no big deal. He had adjusted to this change. He liked his life these days, so much so that he was amused when Donna, one of the supermodels he had dated, passed him in the lobby without giving him a second glance. She still had the capacity to turn heads. The concierge at the front desk sighed in admiration as she disappeared into the building.

"Wouldn't you love the chance to take her out?" he asked wistfully.

"Not me! Nar. Are you kidding? Her kind are full of

their own self-importance, they're not real people at all," he countered in his best down-to-earth country accent.

The moment over, Matt bounced down the steps outside, a little blasé and smug. No one was interested in him these days. He was not important. Looking back over the last months, he had to accept that his excessive defensiveness had been misplaced. He had been an idiot. After all, what the hell did it matter any more? Few people were interested in what had become of him. He had been happily sidelined into the ranks of the forgotten, and that suited him perfectly. He had all he wanted.

He did his usual number of laps in the local swimming pool and even beat his old sports master, who gave up halfway. He then went for a jog along the path by the river before going back to the farm. It had rained, and he was being careful to avoid the puddles.

He was thinking fondly of the beautiful women he had known in London, with their perfectly groomed appearance, the immaculate make-up, the hair and the bright, shiny nails. How would they react to this wonderfully scruffy mechanic and his grubby oil-stained overalls? They would be horrified. Whereas Bridget did not mind at all.

He heard a sudden splash and a shout, and looked around to see a fisherman further upstream waving and pointing to a spot near him. He looked over the edge of the bank to see a boy clinging to one of the remaining supports of the disintegrated jetty, with a larger piece of wood bouncing away. Only last week he had warned some children not to play on the dangerous structure, and here he was seeing what could happen if they did. The child clutching to the upright had begun to slip down the sodden post, and the post itself began to tilt towards the water. Despite a mass of broken branches which had floated into the bank around the spot, the boy and his only lifeline could end up being dragged away together into the middle of the river.

"Damn, damn," he muttered. There was only himself on hand to do anything. Matt had no choice but to wade in, breaking the branches as he slipped in the mud. It only took a few steps through the dirty water to reach the boy and grab him. The pale-faced child clung to him, too shocked to speak, as Matt fought his way back through the branches to the bank. Holding the edge of the bank firmly, he tried to push the boy up to the towpath, but the child would not let go. It was impossible to manage, for he could not let go of his own handhold and lift the boy out at the same time.

The next thing he heard was the siren of a police car coming towards him down the track, no doubt summoned by the fisherman. Its arrival was just in time and soon a big police officer was on the scene and reaching down to yank the boy to safety. Once on the towpath, the officer began checking him over, leaving a wet and filthy Matt to scramble up on his own.

Matt brushed himself down. He flapped his trouser legs to shake the worst of the mud off, took off and emptied his trainers and wrung out his socks before putting them back on. He wriggled his toes inside the damp shoes. It did not feel much better.

Meanwhile the police officer had sat the boy in his car and was obviously phoning the parents. Eventually he returned to Matt.

"That was quick thinking," he said. "The boy is fine, the parents are on their way to collect him."

"It was the angler across the river, over there, who spotted him," said Matt.

"I have his mobile number. I'll talk to him later."

"No one was hurt. Do you need to write this up?" Matt asked.

"I should."

With that, the parents arrived and the policeman went to talk to them. Matt had considered trying to slip away, but the parents did not give him the chance. Full of gratitude, they were soon shaking his hand profusely and he could not escape. He had not done much, he insisted; the fisherman had raised the alarm. He was the one they should be thanking.

Once they had driven off, the policeman turned back to Matt. He had not finished with this passing good Samaritan. He opened his notebook and asked for his name.

"Matthew. Matthew Hillier," he said. There was no need to pretend otherwise.

The man smiled, closed the book and put it in his pocket, asking no more questions. Matt thought this highly odd. The officer then offered to give him a lift home, but Matt insisted he would be fine since he only lived outside the village. He did not mind walking.

"I have a blanket in the boot," said the officer. "You can't walk home like that, in those sopping clothes." He gave him one of those looks that told him he did not have a choice; it would be better for him if he got into the car.

With the blanket wrapped around his legs Matt was driven home, with little said between them, although he sensed that the officer had not finished with him. By the time they had arrived at the farm, the officer still had not spoken. What was going on? Once home, the man leaned across to open the passenger door to let him out. He was beaming broadly.

Matt could see his parents standing perplexed at the window, obviously wondering why he was being brought home in a police car.

"You can relax, Matt. I'm a friend of your Uncle Jim. We used to work together. This report will be diplomatically filed away. I doubt it will see the light of day again. Anything for a local boy."

He chuckled and drove off with a wave. Matt waved back. He knew that the incident would hardly rate more than a few lines in the local paper, even if the fisherman had photos of him on his mobile. He had gone from being terrified of media intrusion to knowing any written words no longer had any influence on him.

He took a quick shower, changed, grabbed his overalls and went off to one of his evening courses. He had contacted various aviation authorities to find out the best way to achieve the necessary professional qualifications. At the moment he was going to the engineering workshop for some practical hands-on experience. Engineering manuals were no substitute for the real thing. He had become obsessed with learning all he could about flying. He wanted to understand how aircraft engines worked; he wanted to fly professionally. This was the future he wanted. His room at home was filling up with the books, catalogues and the flying paraphernalia he needed to study, and it was getting fuller by the day, much to his mother's frustration. She had made no secret of her opinion that the sooner he moved out the better. To think Chris had joked about Bridget's need for extra space, and here he was getting just as bad.

It was also time to start seriously looking for somewhere to live. He would start searching for a place within easy reach of Headcorn Airport, which was where he wanted to be based. He had already negotiated a trial in their workshop. If he was good enough, he hoped for a contract which would allow him to split his time between the engineering side and becoming one of the regular pilots for their small plane charter service. He had had an advantage in the negotiations, since the guys at the airfield already knew him. It was all smiles, and they welcomed his ambition. The friendly atmosphere and working environment promised so much.

Bridget was equally keen for them to find a house and move in together. Until then they would settle for the occasional few days' break somewhere secluded and quiet, where they could just potter about being lazy, smiling and enjoying each other.

Chris had just completed an assignment concerning a factory takeover, where there was a dispute between the management and the union. He had listened to both sides and been totally professional and impartial in his column, something that was second nature to him these days. It was the end of another day in the newsroom, and the three of them went for a drink to unwind before going home.

Alan offered to get everyone another round, but they politely turned him down, begrudgingly accepting that they really should make a move soon.

"Have you noticed they're not doing so many hatchet jobs on celebrities these days?" Alan said.

"About time too. I wish it would stay that way," Chris murmured.

"Nothing in life is perfect, Chris, much as you may want it to be," said Cherry, finishing her drink. "Let's not forget your notes on Francesca Lawson."

Why did she have to keep bringing that up? She seemed to enjoy pointing out his error much too often for Chris's liking. He did not deny that his personal interest in Francesca had been his biggest professional error, one he had been paying for ever since as he kept scanning the tabloids to make sure nothing awful had appeared. He wanted so hard to believe that she was finally safe from public scrutiny. But he was not convinced the papers had been destroyed, either by accident, by the cleaner or someone else. They could still be loitering about somewhere. Damn it!

Chris was in one of his 'get things out of the way' moods. He could never put that right, but he was sure he could find a way to ease the problem if he could talk to Francesca again. Did he deserve to be forgiven? He doubted it. Yet any kind of reconciliation would be a relief. But he was still banned from entering or phoning the Marriott, so how could he see her?

He returned to the internet to see if the hotel group listed any other addresses which might be her private home. Naturally it did not. The organisation was Europe-wide, and even the other board members' names only gave their head office listings. He had to tackle this differently, less obviously. Her parents?

He went back to his copy of the article for the theatre and re-read everything. They owned a cottage in Kent, so there was every possibility that she could escape there when necessary. The land registry, census records and local council index would be useful. It gave him hope. Yep, he was going to follow that up, somehow, in the midst of his normal workload.

That workload was suddenly thrown apart the next day, with the news about the murder of the MP Jo Cox. Gerry was shouting and storming up and down the corridor, bellowing orders for coverage, hard-hitting but sensitive: background, photos, her political career, everything. The whole floor flew into action, and they spent the rest of the morning furiously piecing together the story of the MP's dedicated young life. What was the world coming to?

The news continued to dominate the headlines for a few days before the office settled down again. Then, unexpectedly, Mr Derrick phoned Chris to thank him profusely for the article he had written to undo the harm the other piece had done to his cause. He had only been trying to right a wrong, Chris explained; he did not deserve such praise. Mr Derrick dismissed the protest, saying that Chris's words had been responsible for some wonderful news. His reputation had been restored and an anonymous benefactor had donated a building and some musical instruments to help him to continue his youth schemes. But there was more: the community choir had been invited to sing at the Royal Albert Hall. It was wonderful.

The *Despatch* team needed this good news to lift their spirits. Chris immediately wanted the details. He was going to make a feature of this success, together with photos. That such success had come from the man's hard work deserved to be promoted and bragged about. And he was the person to do it. He would give it all the publicity he could. He was delighted by Mr Derrick's change of fortune. It proved that there really were some good people in this world.

During the morning break, Chris, Cherry and Allan were chatting.

"I heard there is a rumour that the Ryling Coffee campaign is coming back," said Alan.

"Really? I do hope they use the same men in it," said Cherry.

Chris made no comment. He knew there was no way Matt's torso would appear in those pictures again.

"What happened to the one that was injured? He seems to have disappeared off the map."

Chris turned back to his typing. He did not want Cherry to read anything in his expression. She was too sharp by half.

Chris saw a poster for the redevelopment of the mews site previously owned by Captain Tapley, the same man who had owned Aston Hall. He should have ignored it, of course, but it stirred his curiosity. Aston Hall meant Rosie and Jake.

He had long ago discounted Rosie as a witness to anything. She would hardly have stood by and let someone hurt Jake. So where had Jake died? He was still convinced the boy had gone back for the pencils. What if he had seen something he should not have? The house was guarded fiercely by the owner, who perhaps could have been involved in art fraud or stolen property. Had Jake been frightened, then run away and fallen accidentally? Were they worried what he might reveal?

Chris hated the idea that someone might have deliberately killed the boy. His heart was pounding as he fought against the dreadful thought. If it had been an innocent accident, there would have been no need to move him. Putting his body under the tree would have been a diversion to protect themselves, to take attention away from the house, its contents or the guests. Would they be desperate enough to carry Jake to the tree and then coldly leave him for someone else to find? Only the owner could have organised it, knowing how the estate was run. Was he involved? Why had he gone abroad so soon after Jake's death? Were the two things connected? Chris could not believe it was just a coincidence. He decided to head back to the office to check a few dates.

He went back into the newspaper archive website, found the local papers for the year of Jake's death and trawled thorough them. He found the inquest report: accidental death, nothing suspicious.

Cherry returned with a coffee to find Chris staring at the screen. She pulled her chair up next to his.

"What are you up to?"

"Still playing detective," Chris admitted.

"Nothing new there then. You read too many crime novels," she scoffed, before impatiently leaving him to it.

Chris screwed up his eyes, focusing his thoughts. The mystery concerning Jake had developed into a possible crime. What could he do? The police would hardly re-investigate an old accident, as they would see it, from over a decade ago, based purely on his suspicions. They would not take him seriously. Realistically, he had no proof. He did not know which of the men had been there, nor did he have anything to suggest that there were stolen items in the house. Much as he felt he was right, he knew deep down that he could not tell anyone. How could he cause more upset for Rosie, when she had only just forgiven him for the last time?

Then another notion came to mind. Would Rosie's last picture, that bend in the stairs, the window and the painting on the wall, have shown a stolen painting or piece of furniture? What if her drawing held a clue? That was an even more worrying hypothesis.

He sat back in the chair and closed his eyes. He had wanted justice for Jake and his grandfather, but he was not going to get it. He was angry with himself. He had to get a grip. How to shake himself free of his ridiculous obsession? The only way to move on was to concentrate on something else. Anything. Francesca? Was it time to visit Francesca? Why not?

It was a miserably wet evening when he finally arrived at Francesca's home after getting lost several times because of the lack of road names out in the country. He rang the front door bell and prayed she would let him in, although he had no doubt it would only be the once. What he would say would depend on her immediate reaction. He could have the door slammed in his face or at worst be arrested by the police followed by some restraining order and law suit.

The instant change of expression as she saw him on the doorstep told him what to expect, but he knew he had brought this on himself and he had to sort it out, once and for all. He could not back out now.

"You are one damned persistent journalist, Chris Page. I thought we had seen the last of each other. How dare you turn up here? How did you find me?"

"Research. Henry and Jean are both buried in the village churchyard. It seemed logical they would have a home here."

"My, you have been busy," she said sarcastically.

"I have come to apologise again, nothing more. I'm desperately sorry for what I did. I know I had no right to delve into your personal life. It was none of my business."

"Indeed it was not."

"Please, please Francesca. Let me in for a minute."

"It's Miss Lawson to you. And I don't think that is necessary. Your apology is accepted. If that is all, I don't think we have anything else left to say to each other. Do you?"

He had not anticipated being dismissed so quickly.

"I had hoped we could... talk?"

"Why? To make it easier for you? So you could make excuses and walk away with a clear conscience to forget the disaster you could have so easily have caused?"

She looked him up and down disdainfully for what seemed a long time, and shivered in the cold night air. Finally she retreated into the hallway, indicating for him to step inside. She closed the door and reluctantly led him into her warm home. There in the lounge she let him remain standing and began to pace back and forth in front of him. Chris had no doubt that he was in for a rollicking, but he could handle it. He had the measure of her now.

"The fact that none of your inaccurate suggestions have yet to be published is surprising," she sneered. "We both know the press can be ruthless and make the most of the slightest piece of gossip. You people can ruin reputations overnight."

Her eyes blazed and she grinned wickedly. Did he really think she was ignorant of the damage he could have done? Living in London these days, she saw all the shameful revelations in the press. They had a lot to answer for. But she was no fool, she never left anything to chance.

"The disappearance of my research documents still haunts me," said Chris. "I'm sorry. It was never my intention to hurt you."

"Or Oliviero? Just what were your real motives for delving into his life? He has never done anything wrong. Why would you wish to discredit him?"

What could he tell her? The truth? To prevent her being involved in a lengthy doomed relationship with an older and married man, for no other reason than it was his own personal view. That could be dangerous. He chewed his lip briefly and wondered how to answer.

"I do have my own connections, Mr Page. I am aware of the information you accumulated. Were you satisfied with your findings? Was the Rome website useful?"

Chris stared. How could she have found out about that?

Francesca laughed, not a taunting laugh but a relaxed easy natural one, which puzzled him.

"Why was my friendship with Oliviero of any importance?

That he makes special time for me every summer is no secret, either here or in Italy. Neither of us have anything to be ashamed of. I will always love him and I'm glad of every moment we share. He feels the same. There, you can print that and see how many papers it sells." She settled back onto the settee.

Chris winced at her challenge. It was evident that she was completely unconcerned by the prospect of public disclosure and did not care what he thought. That was Italians for you. It was evident from her words that she was still seeing Oliviero, but how he wished she wasn't.

"What did you imagine? Some scandalous behaviour between us?" she went on. "One which would have been well documented across the major tabloids. No, Mr Page, your wild theories would have been of no interest to anyone. I doubt any paper would have been interested. It would hardly be worth two lines on the back page, and it would have been forgotten the next day."

Chris did not understand why she seemed so sure of this. Nor did he understand why she had not ordered him to leave yet. He sighed deeply, his eyes cast to the floor. His visit had resolved nothing. He felt somewhat despondent.

"I'm not that newsworthy in the wider scheme of things," she said. "But what did your research find out about me? Where was I born? Where was I brought up? What schools did I go to?"

"I... er... don't know."

He had concentrated all his efforts on Oliviero; he had

not even thought to try a search on her. Why should he? She was Jean Miller's daughter, that was all he needed to know.

"Mmm. How very unprofessional! I thought you would have been more thorough."

Her curious glance and a slight raise of the eyebrows indicated that she was waiting for some conclusion on his part. "Have you finished here, Mr Page? Did you want anything else?"

"I guess not."

Their conversation seemed to have ended, and Chris saw no point in staying. He had not achieved anything.

"I suppose I had better leave," he said.

"That would be a good idea." She stood up and led him back through the hall, but stopped by one of the other doors.

"Since the Marshall Theatre article was such a glowing tribute, maybe you would like to see some of the private memorabilia Henry Marshall and my mother collected before you go."

He knew he did not deserve this sudden conciliatory gesture on her part after his past behaviour, but he was not about to turn down such an offer.

"Thank you, that's very kind of you."

She led him into a room full of framed theatre and opera posters and paintings. It was a treasure trove of wonderful memories. Other items, sentimental props and postcards of their travels decorated the place, while pieces of china and glass and photos covered the fireplace, bookshelves and piano. He guessed it was her mother Jean's piano; sheets of music sat on the music stand at the side, and a clutter of family photos were arranged on the lid. Here in this hallowed space, he stood overwhelmed by the contents and the warm atmosphere of the room. He had never expected to feel in awe or to feel this sense of insight and admiration for her parents. It was like meeting them in person. He did not want to leave, there was so much to take in.

"This is wonderful," he said.

Francesca smiled in agreement. "Do you like the family photos? What do you think of them?"

He had not dared to look too closely at them, as they were of a more personal and private nature.

"This may be your only chance to see them," she said. "They deserve another glance. They might help you clarify the situation."

Situation? What situation? What was this woman on about? But he studied them closely, as instructed. He found himself looking at several recurring faces. A young man, a young Jean, the pair of them together, a large family group, one of Francesca as a child, then one of Jean and Henry. One of Francesca as a bridesmaid, Francesca with the two young children on holiday in the sun, and a recent portrait of a middle-aged man. One Oliviero Marco Savante. Chris looked at her, puzzled at his picture being displayed so openly here.

"Yes. Oliviero."

She waited for him to say something, but he was silent, his expression blank. Realisation had failed to sink in.

"Well?" she finally asked. "You must want to know why his photo is there."

"It's none of my business."

"Very good, you're learning."

Chris felt a little awkward now. The last thing he wanted was a further intense declaration of her love for this man. He did not want to hear such talk in this room; it would sully this precious place. But he should have known better than to second guess anything connected with Francesca.

"There's no reason why I should put you out of your misery, Mr Page, but it seems I have to. You only have half the story. I really can't believe you are that dim. These are my family photos, isn't it obvious? Are you oblivious to the link? Oliviero is my father. A loving father, who makes special time for me, especially in the summer."

Chris's mouth dropped open, astounded at her proud declaration. He stood there, staring from her, back to the photos and back to her again. No way, that was impossible!

"You don't believe me. Why do you think I speak such fluent Italian as well as English?"

"But your surnames are different," he mumbled.

"Lawson is just a name I use for convenience, to avoid the curious." Her mouth crinkled slightly.

He wanted to ask more, but he did not think it was appropriate. How could he have got this so wrong?

"He married my mother before they went their own ways, lived their own lives. Their relationship got in the way of their different ambitions. I spent most of my childhood in Milan, living a normal Italian family life, safe from the publicity surrounding my famous mother. When she was resting I spent time with her, usually in quiet locations like her villa in Sardinia. They both remarried happily and I had two sets of caring families to spend my life with. Jean and Henry settled here when she retired. They were perfect together, I loved them dearly, just as I love my father, Martha and my two half-brothers. My father is my father after all," she added softly, full of warm affection.

Chris would have liked to sit down to absorb all this information, but he managed to stay on his feet. He could also do with a drink, but none was on offer. That was the last thing he had expected to find out by coming here tonight.

His brain was analysing his original finding. That they met in private places to be alone together did not mean so much now. Her relationship with this Oliviero had not been that much of a secret in Sardinia. The villagers had never raised an eyebrow or expressed any concern about her reputation. Instead, this small community had all been part of a silent, loyal conspiracy to protect her and her father. He could see that, in hindsight. He had let her get under his skin. When discussing the Marshall Theatre with her, he had assumed that Henry was her father. Why would he think differently? There had been no reason to. Another mistake.

Finally his mind came back to the present. He was still here, looking at her, his mind considering what he had learned. When he had confessed to losing those papers, she had not put him right; instead she had deliberately let him punish himself unnecessarily. Hadn't he tried to put it right at the station and later at her office? She could have stopped this earlier, but she had not. She had deliberately played him and made him pay. All this time, all these months of tense uncertainty and worry had been unnecessary. She must have revelled in knowing how he had tormented himself. He was stunned that she had been that cruel, and suddenly angry with her. The idea of some therapeutic absolution had vanished. He hated this woman. Damn her!

"Did you enjoy making me suffer?" he asked harshly.

"You did that to yourself, you only have yourself to blame. You were the one who had the nerve to jump to the wrong conclusions and put it down on paper."

Chris wanted to argue; his actions had been a mistake and not done maliciously, while her actions were the opposite, deliberately deceitful and wicked. He had been taken in by the charming aura she had created. In fact she had turned out to be a manipulative, devious, mean-minded bitch! He pushed his tongue into his cheek to stop him from saying it.

"I admit I had thought better of you Mr Page. I had been told you were good at your job, that you were quite perceptive. Yet on this occasion, you cannot deny that your research was ridiculously inadequate. It would have been easy enough to find out Oliviero was my father if you had looked in the right places." She gave a self-satisfied smirk. "Goodbye, Mr Page."

That was all he remembered her saying as he left.

Back home, now he knew the truth about Oliviero and Francesca, he was still seething. All that time he had wasted worrying about her, worrying over the detrimental effect it would have on her if the papers had printed anything, and she hadn't given a tinker's cuss about him or the stress he had endured. What was more annoying was the realisation that she had obviously had enough influence to squash any damning articles if necessary, right from the start.

He had gone there to apologise, hoping to be forgiven. Instead, as far as he was concerned, she should have apologised to him. Just maybe that was the way she had been brought up, to do anything to protect herself and her father from the inquisitive world, but that was no excuse. He was not going to forgive her. He wanted payback, he wanted to wipe that smirk off her face. How dare she think she could do as she pleased, disregarding other people's lives?

But as his anger subsided, he knew there was no point in engaging in a battle of words with her. It was not worth it; he would only get more wound up. He knew when to walk away, hard as it was.

Cherry would never believe what he had to tell her about Francesca, if he ever told her. At the moment he was inclined not to mention his visit at all. He was not in the mood to be moaned at and be called stupid again. And if Cherry ever mentioned Francesca again, she would wish she hadn't. In fact he did not want to talk to anyone for a while; he wanted to be left alone to re-evaluate his life. His instinct had been so far off beam. Maybe it was time to stop being a journalist, if he was making such a mess of things. But no, that was silly. He was just a little weary.

He was determined to regain his composure. He made himself a promise. He must learn not to waste his energy on his insane nosiness and impossible thoughts. He was also going to alter the way he dealt with the news and not get bogged down when important national politics reared its ugly head, with the ensuing passionate debates and arguments. He took the UK's vote to leave the EU and David Cameron's resignation as Prime Minister in his stride. His personal views on the subject were tempered almost to indifference.

The only thing to frustrate Chris's plan to stay detached from further problems was Bridget's enquiring mind. He had idly been looking out of the window when she came up behind him and laid her chin on his shoulder.

"Christopher," she purred.

"What?"

He turned round, and was immediately was suspicious at her soft puppy-dog expression. What did she want to wheedle out of him?

"I was wondering about Matt's accident," she said. "He always said it was a simple accident, that he had been knocked down in a car park, But, no one ever talks about it."

He cringed. Had she suddenly latched on to this, because like him, she had suspected there was more to this accident?

"It seems odd," she said.

"Not necessarily."

They both knew Matt had been seriously injured and had attended an excessive number of hospital appointments, but no one had made a fuss. Why should they?

"Where did that come from, after all this time?" he asked.

"I saw his scars. They were more than I would expect from being hit by a car."

Chris raised his eyebrows, widened his eyes and gave her one of those frowns. It was obvious their relationship had become more intimate than he had realised. He was tempted to tease her, but refrained. She did not even blush or seem embarrassed. She was too intent on her question.

"I can't ask Matt. It might stir up painful memories."

"Then why do you need to know? Surely it's better left alone."

"Would you ask Mike about it? Please. I don't like to."

"Are you serious?" Chris was shocked at her suggestion.

She nodded.

"Please try, Chris. Please."

"It's not a good idea."

She hugged him, but all the hugs in the world could not convince him that he would do this. He was worried. He was going to phone Paula first to see what she could do to talk Bridget out of this madness. His dear younger sister should not expect miracles.

CHAPTER 12

The last thing Chris was going to do was to ask Mike what had happened. He preferred to warn him, and subsequently Matt, of the problem.

"I'm sorry about this Mike, but Bridget has a bee in her bonnet about Matt's accident. She suddenly want to know more. I don't know why."

Mike expelled a great sigh of frustration. His tone was serious.

"The truth is that Matt was in the wrong place at the wrong moment," he said. "A few minutes later and it might never have happened. Maybe if we had left the restaurant together... but then life is full of maybes and what ifs."

He did not clarify anything else, but Chris could sense a regret in the words, as if Mike almost blamed himself.

"Matt would not like Bridget to learn the details," Mike went on. "His injuries were hard enough for him to deal with. And the cause of them is still hard to accept," he added sadly.

"I understand," Chris murmured, and the conversation ended.

And Chris really did understand. That Matt wanted to protect Bridget and himself from something really bad. He was not sure he wanted to know the rest anyway. He was content to remain ignorant. It was easier.

Chris was not sure what he was going to say to Bridget, no doubt she expected him to have answers.

"I haven't spoken to Mike yet," he lied.

"That's all right. You don't need to now. Paula told me off for being irrational. She convinced me I was being silly. If it's better I don't know, then I accept that. I don't want him to dwell on it. I want us to be happy. And if that means never talking about it, then that's how it will be. I have to think of him," she chirped in her normal carefree manner.

He had not expected this sudden turnaround; he could not believe that Paula had made her see sense. Bridget was not usually persuaded this easily.

"Are you OK with that? Can you manage that?" he asked. He was quite doubtful. He stared at his sister.

"Oh yes, easily. Besides, if he hadn't had that accident, I would never have met him as I did."

Bridget went on to admit that nothing was going to spoil

her future with Matt. She intended to enjoy every day as it came; she had so much to look forward to.

Matt was a lucky man, Chris decided. *Thank you, Paula,* he mouthed as Bridget left.

With that out of the way, Chris was surprised by Matt's arrival the next day. He had had no warning that he was coming. Nevertheless he was the welcoming host, jovial and pleased to see him.

"Come on in, make yourself at home," he said. But he was puzzled when Matt made his way into the house and sat down.

Matt had finished his first week at the aerodrome's service facility, working his fingers to the bone, when Mike dropped the bombshell about Bridget's question. Matt had to consider his best course of action. It was in Bridget's own interests to have her inquisitiveness stopped. He had to talk to Chris; he could not let the problem become insurmountable. He had finally conquered the fear, but he still could not speak of it out loud. He remembered those early months when the demons had returned. The pain, his own screams echoing so loudly in his head, drowning out everything. Mike's ashen face and people running, shouting, figures and lights. The hospital, his parents. The nights he had battled through the flashbacks and panic attacks and buried himself in dark places to shut it out, until the nightmares had subsided. He hated what had happened. No one should share that, especially Bridget. But how to make Chris understand that without telling him why?

"You phoned Mike. I really want to keep Bridget ignorant. For my sake as well as hers," said Matt.

To see him look so downcast and solemn revealed the effort it took for him just to think about that awful night. Yet Chris's quick response quickly put him out of his misery.

"Matt, you can stop worrying. The crisis is over, Bridget won't be pursuing this."

"You're sure?" Matt's eyes widened in disbelief. He had not expected the problem to vanish so easily.

"Oh yes. Bridget cares too much to risk hurting you," Chris reassured him.

"Thank you. Thank you for whatever you said to her," Matt gushed.

Chris could hear the relief in his voice. "It's not me you should thank. Paula was the one worked the miracle."

Chris settled Matt down in an armchair opposite, to let him recover himself. His old confidence soon returned when Chris asked him how his new career plans were progressing. He could not have cheered him any more than by asking that question. Matt confessed that he wanted to combine being a top-class aircraft mechanic with actually flying planes. He already had a pilot's licence for small planes, which had prompted his nickname 'Kite' amongst the rugby team. He had completed his refresher course and would be based at Headcorn Airfield. The company which ran the aerodrome were willing to subsidise the rest of his specialised mechanical training, as they were keen to have him as a permanent fixture in the workforce. They had also added his name to the list of charter pilots they used for private hire. They had three planes for hire and when they were not in use, he would be flying them to keep them in running order.

He stopped to smile. Everything was going really well. One day he hoped to become a flying instructor. He also admitted he had always fancied being a helicopter pilot as well, but one thing at a time. "Aircraft, helicopters and machinery were always my passions on the farm when growing up," he said. He had so many plans, and he was beaming with enthusiasm. He was happy to share his dreams with a sympathetic listener, and Chris could not help being impressed by his growing ambition. He admired his determination. He could see that there would be no stopping him. Yes, Matt was special.

Maybe that feeling of pure, ecstatic happiness had rubbed off on Chris. For some unknown reason he had spent the weekend actually doing the painting he had been putting off for well over six months. He found it was not as tedious as he had imagined, nor did it take as long as he had expected, and now the brushes were clean and all the tins and rags had been placed in their correct storage space in the shed; he had even tidied the shelves. He had simply woken up yesterday morning and set to work. It had been quite therapeutic. Now he felt immensely satisfied and good in himself. His house was tidy, bright and sparkling.

Even Bridget was impressed when she called in. "Are you expecting someone special?" she joked.

"You're special, aren't you?" he replied.

She screwed up her nose and grinned, then hugged and kissed him, for no other reason than that he was her dearest brother. Her only brother.

Chris had a personal interest in covering a fundraising event at the Palace Hotel. Bridget had been responsible for the presentation artwork and the accompanying exhibition, so he was keen for their photographer to take plenty of shots, his idea being that they could be passed on to Bridget for her portfolio. He watched her mix with the public, working the room for new clients. A bigwig of some sort was showing some interest, so he hung back to wait until Bridget was finished. He wanted a quick word with her before he left to put the column to print, but it looked like he was going to have to settle for just a wave instead, since she was still in conversation.

He overheard the man say that he had seen her being dropped off by Matt Hillier. Bridget simply smiled, without elaborating.

"I'm pleased he has recovered so well," said the man. Again she smiled and nodded, giving nothing away.

Then Nathan, their press photographer, sidled up to Chris and nudged him.

"Is your sister stepping out with 'Kite' Hillier?" he asked furtively.

There was no point in denying it; Nathan had been with Chris when Bridget arrived earlier.

"That's a nice old-fashioned phrase," Chris replied. "But the whole world doesn't need to know. And certainly no one in our own press office."

"OK, I get the message." Nathan grinned.

Chris had always liked Nathan; the two of them had often worked together and he had excelled himself helping Mrs Cooper with her shop. He was definitely a decent guy.

"How long have Bridget and Matt been seeing each other?" he asked.

"Since last summer."

"Wow! Well good luck to them."

Bridget called in at the weekend as usual.

"Who was the suit you were chatting to at the charity event?" Chris asked her.

"Some famous surgeon. I didn't get his name."

Chris let the topic drop, not wanting her to draw her attention to the link he had just made. The surgeon's comment concerning Matt indicated that he might have been part of the medical team that had operated on him. That could have been a close call; who knew what else might have been said?

Nathan popped round the following evening on his way across town, to drop off the contact sheet of photos for Bridget. Nathan said there was no rush to let him know which ones she wanted printing, and then almost too casually confided that he had known Matt as a child.

"It was only a vague acquaintance," he said. "I played on his farm as a kid during the holidays, when my grandparents worked there."

Talk about coincidences, but Nathan had nothing else to add.

Nathan had duly completed Bridget's order, which left Chris taking him for a drink at lunchtime as an extra thank you.

"Those photos for her portfolio were really good," Chris said.

"I enjoy my work. I always want to produce the best I can."

Nathan was quite laid back about the praise, no doubt because he knew his own worth; his photos were taken with care for the subject. After chatting to Chris about a variety of topics, he returned to the subject of Matt.

"I can't believe they never caught the sods responsible for his injuries. How could anyone do that to another human being?"

It was clear Nathan knew a lot more about the incident than was generally known. Maybe he assumed that both Bridget and Chris must know, which was why he talked so freely.

"I don't suppose anyone mentions the cause of his injuries," Nathan went on. "Let's face it, why should they? It must be an awful burden for him to live with."

Chris made no comment.

"You might as well know, my uncle was one of the few witnesses who saw the whole thing take place," Nathan went on. "He was an accountant for the restaurant. He had been working upstairs in the office and was looking out of the window. Who would have imagined such a thing? That when Matt challenged some men breaking into cars, instead of walking away, they turned on him."

"What?" Chris could not help himself reacting, although Nathan did not notice. Not an 'accident' then, Chris silently concluded.

"Unfortunately they couldn't be identified from that distance. They were just three shadows in the dark who ran away leaving Matt on the ground. I heard they beat his leg to a pulp with an iron bar. No one will confirm it, no one wants to. He could have lost his lower leg. It was too brutal, too brutal to be believed. It was a terrible night for everyone."

"Yes," Chris managed to answer. He was swallowing hard to control his own shock. This was worse than he had imagined. No wonder no one talked about it. That phrase 'beaten to a pulp' echoed around his head for the rest of their lunch break before they parted.

Chris could not stop thinking about it. He did not sleep much that night. He could not imagine the sheer agony Matt must have suffered, although he was trying not to think about it. The thought of his leg being smashed and splintered made him feel sick. Such a horrendous, senseless attack by those vicious thugs, and then to endure endless surgery afterwards. It made him shudder. His poor family – no wonder no one talked about it. Self-preservation came to mind.

Chris's attention returned to the restaurant where it had happened. The words 'collision' and 'incident' had been used in the official account. After the shock and outrage at the attack on Matt in the car park the restaurant had been targeted by the media for information, but the staff had remained silent about that night ever since. Now Chris knew why those around him refuse to talk about it. including his team mates. There was no doubt Matt was protected by a growing circle of people, some of whom did not know him personally. Their loyalty amazed him. Now he had to join that band.

Poor Bridget. Then it dawned on Chris that Nathan could unintentionally let the cat out of the bag when casually talking to her. Bridget had to be saved from this. He could not have her accidentally finding out about that fateful night. Hellfire! He would have to have a word with Nathan first thing tomorrow to prevent that happening.

Chris came to work early. He found Nathan in the newsroom, took him aside and explained that Bridget was completely ignorant of the cause of the attack and he would prefer she remained so. Nathan naturally understood and promised to keep the secret from her. He did not usually talk about it; it was only because he assumed Chris had seemed to know, that he had ventured to say anything.

"I think his brother and his team blamed themselves for not leaving the restaurant at the same time as he had," said Nathan. "If they had he might never have been attacked. I can't imagine they will ever forget the sight of finding him like that. They were all stunned."

Chris remembered what Mike had said about Matt being in the wrong place at the wrong time. No wonder Mike had sounded so regretful.

"With no CCTV on the car park, no one could identify the culprits," said Nathan. "They never caught the bastards responsible. Not even the Metropolitan Police or his brother could find them. Lack of evidence, I suppose. I expect Matt still resents the fact those men were never caught."

Chris nodded. What else could he do? He wanted to offer some participation in this conversation, to hide his ignorance. What? Something general, perhaps.

"He never talks about it," Chris muttered.

No one seemed to notice Chris's quietness at work over the next few days, and no one there would have suspected the real reason. He wished he had never been told, that he had never found out. He was plagued by his thoughts. Everything else had paled in insignificance. It was no wonder it was hard to concentrate on his work.

Here was Matt, a typical country boy, who had tasted success, been an international sports star, travelling the world and mixed with the social elite, and been the toast of the town. He had lost his career and had gone back to an ordinary life without any complaint. To all appearances there was nothing extraordinary about him. There was nothing to indicate what he had been.

Chris could only hope he could appear normal himself when he met Matt next time. The easy friendship already established between them should work in his favour. In fact, he had been amazed at his own ability to keep eye contact and remain light-hearted when the three of them met at Bridget's house.

They gathered the next weekend to help clear out of some of Bridget's junk. About time! The boxes of broken china she had accumulated since she had started her new hobby, Kintsugi, had not helped. Kintsugi was the art of repairing broken china with 'golden joinery', and she had put the boxes aside to be closely guarded. Therefore, as Bridget emptied the other boxes out on the floor, it became apparent that her idea of sorting the contents was nothing like what Chris and Matt had imagined. There was a lot of teasing, with both of them asking her if that was *all* she intended to throw out. They had expected more.

"You were right," Matt acknowledged.

Bridget frowned at them and let it go without comment. She wasn't really bothered how much or little she got rid of, because since she had decided to keep her house in in London as a useful base, it was clearly going to give her leverage in what she kept. But her home would be with Matt, wherever that might be, and she promised not to take too much with her. The boys both laughed, they didn't believe that.

After less than an hour the sorting-out had come to a halt, leaving a mess of unclassified articles across the lounge while they all sat pulling faces at the lack of progress. They had all had enough and Bridget, yawning, settled on the settee with Matt plonking down beside her. Chris smiled at the sight of them together. Their fondness and familiarity with each other were evident, regardless of having an audience. He noticed how comfortably Matt held Bridget's hand and gave it a gentle squeeze now and again.

After a much-needed coffee and a sandwich, Chris left them to it and softly closed the front door behind him, relieved that he had managed to keep his fresh knowledge hidden. It had not been that hard when they had all been engaged in their usual banter. He should not have worried. Could he keep it up? Would it become easier in the future?

With Bridget and Matt off to look at another property, Mike and Chris went for a drink together, hoping to find somewhere with live music. Since Mike knew all about Chris and his sister's association with the Aston Hall estate, he had no hesitation in bringing up a curious development which he thought Chris might be interested in hearing about. He mentioned that Interpol had recently made a request to investigate the contents of the Hall. Some experts had come over to search the interior.

"From my visit inside the place, it was like a museum,

dull and dusty. What were they looking for? Did they find anything interesting?" asked Chris. He was intrigued about the house and its contents, especially after theorising about its use at the time of Jake's accident.

Mike gave an exaggerated shrug, widened his eyes and grinned. Then in the voice of Manuel from 'Fawlty Towers', he said, "Don't ask me. I know *nothing*."

Chris scrutinised Mike's face, wondering if he was hinting the opposite.

"No honestly, that's all I know. The results of international police investigations remained confidential and restricted, even to us. But I will let you know if I hear anything else." Mike grinned.

Naturally their conversation eventually turned to discussing their siblings. Matt was getting to grips with his new career, one which had come as a bolt out of the blue, Mike admitted. And as for Bridget, her business was growing by the day. It was a wonder they could balance everything they wanted to do. This house search was continuing; who would have thought it would take so long? Chris knew it was nothing to do with the prices, because Matt must have got megabucks for his exclusive luxury flat in Richmond. They just wanted to find the right place. A forever home.

As the hours drifted by they found themselves discussing Woody Guthrie, his life and influence. They had both seen a television documentary and had been impressed by the legacy of his songs. It had been an eye opener, as they had known so little about him. For once the television had produced a great programme, rather than the usual mundane rubbish.

After another drink, Mike leaned forward, changing the topic completely.

"You never asked about Matt's accident," he said.

"Why should I? You indicated it was best left."

Chris was going to have to do his utmost to pretend he did not know what he did. He was going to have to lie as convincingly as he could. This was a policeman with years of training he was facing. He hoped he would be good enough.

"Honestly, it's better Bridget doesn't know. It is not easy to live with," Mike continued.

Chris could not, would not ever forget what he had been told by Nathan. Yet Mike was looking at him, studying his face and working out what he read there. Then he nodded. "But somehow, you know this."

Chris did not answer, not wishing to betray the extent of his knowledge. How could he show empathy for something he was not supposed to know about? He tried not to look away; that would be too obvious. He hoped Mike could not tell that the truth had already changed him. He did not know what he could say to this man.

"How long have you known?" said Mike.

"I know *nothing*," Chris replied, trying his own impression of Manuel.

Of course, Mike did not believe him. He raised an eyebrow, knowing instinctively it was a lie. Chris did not fool him for a minute; he probably knew all of it. His eyes were a giveaway, despite the straight face. As an experienced police officer, Mike appreciated his determination keep silent. How he had found out did not matter, as it was perfectly clear it would go no further. He accepted that he could trust Chris without even having to ask for his promise.

There was no need to say anything more between them.

"I think I owe you another drink," Mike offered.

"That would be appreciated."

Mike put the drinks down. He looked into his glass and then at Chris.

"Ok, I wasn't going to tell you, but I think it might help if you understood the rest. After the attack, Matt hated the men for changing his life and the world for letting it happen. There were days when you couldn't talk to him. His face was like thunder. There was so much fire raging inside him. He had become a different person, he clammed up. It was hard to get through to him. He was fighting his nightmares, his fear and his pain.

"Once he was home on the farm, there was nowhere to hide from Mum and Dad's determined campaign to channel his recuperation. There was no chance to sit around and mope. They didn't make it easy for him. He moaned a lot, but it didn't get him anywhere."

"So why all the secrecy about the attack? None of the public discovered even a whiff of the truth."

"We thought it best to keep the details under wraps. Who would it help to broadcast the details everywhere? Why let the media create a furore of publicity? Matt was in his darkest period, he couldn't handle the attention. Most people respected the request to keep stum, and then later there was no wish to talk about it."

"Thank goodness his life has turned around for the better at last," said Chris.

CHAPTER 13

The weeks were flying by. Bridget had a new project to work on, a seaside theme, which occupied much of her spare time. Naturally with that and Matt, she began missing the normal Friday or weekend catch-ups with him. Chis could see that their routine was slowly changing, not that he minded. All the signs were there; Bridget would still be in touch, but she not as much. Life was moving on, as it should. It was a shame his wasn't.

Then an excited phone call from his cousin Callum interrupted his thoughts. A loud whoop of joy bounced into his ear. He had been offered a post in Canada, even before taking his final exams. He was going to Toronto. He was coming down to London, to the Canadian Embassy, the next weekend to fill in the required documentation, which naturally meant he wanted to scrounge a bed overnight – again. Chris did not even think to refuse, even as a joke. Callum was on cloud nine, and it would have gone over his head. Here was his cousin also moving on with his life. Chris was beginning to feel stagnant, left behind and… old. He looked at his face in the mirror. But he was not that old!

Chris was sent to cover the story of a house fire in East London. Were they really that short of news to send out a senior reporter? What was the editor thinking? He did not like such stories, but he did as he was told. He was grateful the scene had not been too awful, with no harrowing fatalities. He followed his usual procedure of talking to the neighbours to find out the background of the occupant. He discovered that the man had been a newspaperman originally, but had lost his job and had been reduced to stacking shelves in the local supermarket on a very low income. Chris made no comment.

The investigating fire officer added more to the story. Since the man had seemed to be struggling financially, they had not ruled out the theory that the fire was deliberate and possibly an insurance job. It was now suspected arson, and the owner was being held at the police station for questioning.

There was nothing else relevant to alert Chris's interest and he returned to the office, where he wrote a straightforward report and left it at that. It was nothing out of the ordinary.

Alan, however, on listening to the story, wanted to do some more digging. He was like a dog with a bone, and beginning to turn into another version of Chris, full of questions and theories. Chris had no objection to him doing a follow-up if he wanted. He really no longer cared. What happened to journalists in the end? They worked their socks off until they retired with little thanks, or took redundancy to find some peaceful cottage to grow old in. Then they were never heard of again. Did he want that fate?

The day ended with Chris in a deeply reflective mood, a mood which accompanied him home.

What had he achieved? What had he done in life that made a difference? Nothing. He had not made any major contribution or scooped any earth-shattering revelations. The many sad, bad, doom and gloom sensational news items seemed to outnumber the bright, happy moments. What with the air crash into the Mediterranean in May and the recent terrorist attack in Nice on Bastille Day in July, there was definitely more bad news than good. He was just another man telling stories to sell papers. For whose benefit? In the scheme of things he was not special, like Matt, who had battled through so many difficulties and was proudly starting a new life. How Chris envied his courage.

Chris was dissatisfied with himself. He was not happy. He sat in his armchair for a long time that evening, considering his own perception of the world and himself. His enquiring mind had been a necessary requirement for his job, but had his inquisitiveness just become a mind-set he had fallen into over the years out of habit? Had it taken over? It had definitely got out of hand on two memorable occasions. So much for being a professional journalist! His life had become – well, he wasn't sure.

He went to pour himself a glass of wine to shake off the sweet voice of reason which had whispered the answer in his ear. Then he fell asleep on the settee

He woke with a stiff neck. Yawning, he shuffled into the kitchen, where the sun hurt his eyes as he made breakfast. He didn't even bother to shower and change. He leaned on the kitchen window sill, staring at the blue sky and the garden and watching the birds. Mesmerised, he let the time pass, having decided he did not have to rush to do anything in particular today.

He had done a lot of soul-searching last night, until sudden clarity had hit him. He had suddenly had enough. He did not need to keep on being good at his job or proving himself to others. He had nothing to prove to himself. He did not need this job. Today he was going to be spontaneous, which was completely out of character. He needed new challenges, to make more of himself. And why not? He could do this! He had decided he wasn't the only one who was going to make a fresh start.

He wrote a letter, then signed it, put it in his pocket and made his way into the office. There he wandered casually through the building and went to talk to Gerry, his Editor in Chief. He was offered an immediate pay rise to persuade him to stay, but it did not work. He already felt different. In his office, he looked at his computer screen, the printers and phones and the paperwork scattered across all the desks. Did it matter anymore? Should it? Anyone could do this job; it just wasn't going to be him any more. He let out a satisfied sigh.

Chris waited until both Alan and Cherry were in the office before he made his big announcement.

"I have put my notice in. As of now, I've quit the newspaper business. I'm using up the rest of my annual leave so I can walk out of the door today."

Alan and Cherry stopped what they were doing and stared in shock. They could not believe what he had said. Speechless at first, they soon found their voices. Was he serious? Was he mad? Why? How could he give it all up? What would he do?

On a personal level, Cherry was horrified. She had not seen this coming. He had never complained about being that dissatisfied. She thought she knew him after all their years of close association; she knew his moods and his frustration. She had an insight into how he thought, although recently she had begun to wonder. He had not been telling her everything. His unexpected visit to Francesca's home had concerned her. She had not known of his plans, or how he had discovered her parents' home address. There had been nothing she could do to prevent him, and he had never told her about it, even after the event.

Was his leaving her own self-inflicted private punishment, for not telling Chris that she and Francesca had been close friends since they were children at boarding school? Cherry had known all about his altercation with her in Sardinia; she had known his every confrontation. Although he had not told her about all of them, Francesca had.

Cherry had been the perfect spy in his office. She had never let Francesca down. Cherry had done her best to minimise the research information about Olivier that she had passed to Chris. To protect her friend's privacy, her Italian translation had been very selective, which was why his research was deliberately inadequate. No one had been aware of her confidential phone calls warning Francesca what Chris was doing. And it was she who had destroyed the documents Chris had lost. Francesca had been in control the whole time.

Francesca did what she had always done. 'Don't put up with any nonsense' she had been told by her father, and she never had. It was habit. She had persuaded Cherry to pass on copies of Chris's information about the owner of Aston Hall, his art gallery and the names of his partners. Why waste his research, Francesca insisted, when it might be useful for her father? Which it had been. Oliviero had recovered items from his own missing family treasure from years ago via Interpol. She had told Cherry how one vase had strangely contained some dusty pencils wrapped in a now threadbare boy's handkerchief. What a shame the contents had not been more valuable, she had joked. But this was no joke; Cherry would have to accept that Chris was leaving.

But Cherry had another secret; she had always been secretly, and hopelessly, in love with Chris. She had given up waiting for him to notice her as anything except a colleague, and now she would see him no more. They had been a good team and he had been a good friend. She would miss him terribly.

She studied Chris's happy face, knowing there was no way she could persuade him to stay. This was the end of an era. No more chats on the journey to and from work, no more popping into the coffee shop or the local pub. And worse, he might not even come to the houseboat to share social gatherings with her artisan friends. Life would not be the same.

"Are you sure?" she asked again.

Chris nodded and gave a wide smile of utter contentment. He was perfectly satisfied. He told them he had no idea what he would do, he wasn't going to make plans. He was going to enjoy each day as it came.

The rest of the team could not believe he would give it all up as simply as that, with no future plans and no semblance of a job lined up. Had he abandoned all common sense? This was Chris, not some free-spirited hippy. What had come over him?

It took him only a few minutes to clear his desk. He simply tipped most of the clutter into the waste bin. There was nothing important or sensitive on his computer; the information concerning Aston Hall, the owner and his partners, were of little use to anyone. Unless Alan found out about Interpol's interest in the contents of Aston Hall, then that was up to him. It was not Chris's concern any more.

He walked out of the office with head held high and feeling immensely calm. He had not even decided what to do with the rest of the day. There was nothing special on his mind. He went for a walk to the park, picked up a take-away coffee and a newspaper and headed for a bench where he could sit and people-watch. He took in a deep breath and let it out slowly. He really had let go.

In front of him was an idyllic scene; children playing, couples strolling and families picnicking. People were passing the time of day with strangers and stopping to make a fuss of dogs. The world looked different to him today. He sat there taking it all in, smiling as pleasant daydreams and idle fancies danced around his head. He was going to wait and see how he felt later. A lot later. He had to get used to this new approach to life first.

He smiled to himself. He could not stop a myriad different ideas bursting into his imagination – not that he was going to make any rash decisions. With his new laid-back attitude he readily accepted that if one plan did not come to fruition, he would move onto the next. It did not matter what he did.

He realised that he needed just one person in his life

now: Ellen. Maybe there was something special they could work on together. Wouldn't that be something...

In this mellow mood Chris walked slowly home from the park, taking in the beautiful day. And it was a beautiful day, in every respect. He stopped at his front door, looking at it fondly. Home. He loved his small terraced house. It was still full of her stuff, and held so many reminders of the things they had shared together. It was just waiting for her to complete it again. And to think he had briefly contemplated renting out their home, if he had to work away. How could he? What would Ellen think if she came home to find someone else there disturbing their precious belongings? And it *was* their home; it belonged to them, no one else.

He opened the front door, and heard something he had not expected; the radio. Then he heard another sound; running water. The shower was being used upstairs. And at the foot of the stairs sat a battered old-fashioned rucksack...

He knew that rucksack. It was Ellen's. She was home.

He closed the door quietly and stood there holding his breath. He could not describe the way he felt; it was wonderful. And then he heard footsteps on the stairs, and those lovely long legs appeared as she walked down the stairs to greet him, rubbing her damp, tousled hair with a towel. The look in her eyes told him all he needed to know.

"It's been a long time," he said.

"Too long. My fault," she said softly.

"I missed you," he whispered, although it did not need

saying. His heart swelled as she took his hand and he closed his fingers around hers. She kissed him.

They had such a lot to catch up on, but not until he had cooked her breakfast, even this late in the day. Nothing had changed, and as she sat there in his borrowed sweatshirt and pyjama bottoms, he knew this was how it was meant to be.

Later she lay comfortably in his arms, as if she had never been away. They lay nestled together again in contented silence, her soft touch resting on him in that familiar special way. Neither of them had forgotten the smallest detail of each other. Chris's whole being cherished this woman. She was everything to him. She made him complete. The calm understanding, the silent understanding between them, their fondness for each other. This was all he wanted, all that was important. He could breathe properly again.

"You're smiling," she whispered without moving.

Held in her blissful embrace, he smiled even more. Ellen had come back.

"I quit my job," he whispered.

She sighed forgivingly, rolled onto her side, brushed his hair back from his face, looking him straight in the eyes, her eyes twinkling.

"Good."

Epilogue

A year had passed since their reunion and Chris and Ellen were on holiday, lazing on a long and largely deserted sandy beach, enjoying the sun and listening to the soft rippling of the waves. Relaxed and utterly at peace with himself, Chris reflected on the year that had passed since her return.

Their home and family life was much the same. They had not found a common project to work on together as he had imagined, but that did not matter. Ellen had returned to the research facility of the university and he was still having the occasional night out with Mal and Tom, as he searched for a fresh career. The rest of the family were intact; Bridget and Matt were happily settled in their charming red brick period country cottage *with* outbuildings. Callum was building a career in Canada and young Rosie was in her element at horticultural college, taking a degree in botany.

Chris had never been unemployed for long, as he tried different opportunities. He had turned down a job as a roving television reporter, despite the high wages. He had worked at a printers, with ink, oil and machinery as his constant tools, before his love of books and people had him working in Mrs Cooper's magical book shop for a while. Here a chance meeting with the customer Stefan had turned his prospects around. Stefan suggested a job in radio, something Chris had never envisaged. Why would he? He knew nothing about radio. Initially hired as a general assistant, he soon moved on to the more technical aspects of the business. The whirlwind learning curve of tackling the whole challenge of his startling employment had surprised him. Who knew what was next?

Ellen ran her fingers through his thick hair, and Chris opened his bright blue eyes to smile at her. They smiled at each other a lot. Life was what it was; he would not have it any other way. It was just like old times, doing crazy things together. Next year they planned get an old camper van, do it up and mooch about exploring the countryside, every chance they could. He chuckled at the thought of revisiting their youth and repeating some of their former adventures.

"The world has so much more to offer," said Ellen.

He knew she was right.

BV - #0060 - 140722 - C0 - 203/127/16 - PB - 9781861518804 - Gloss Lamination